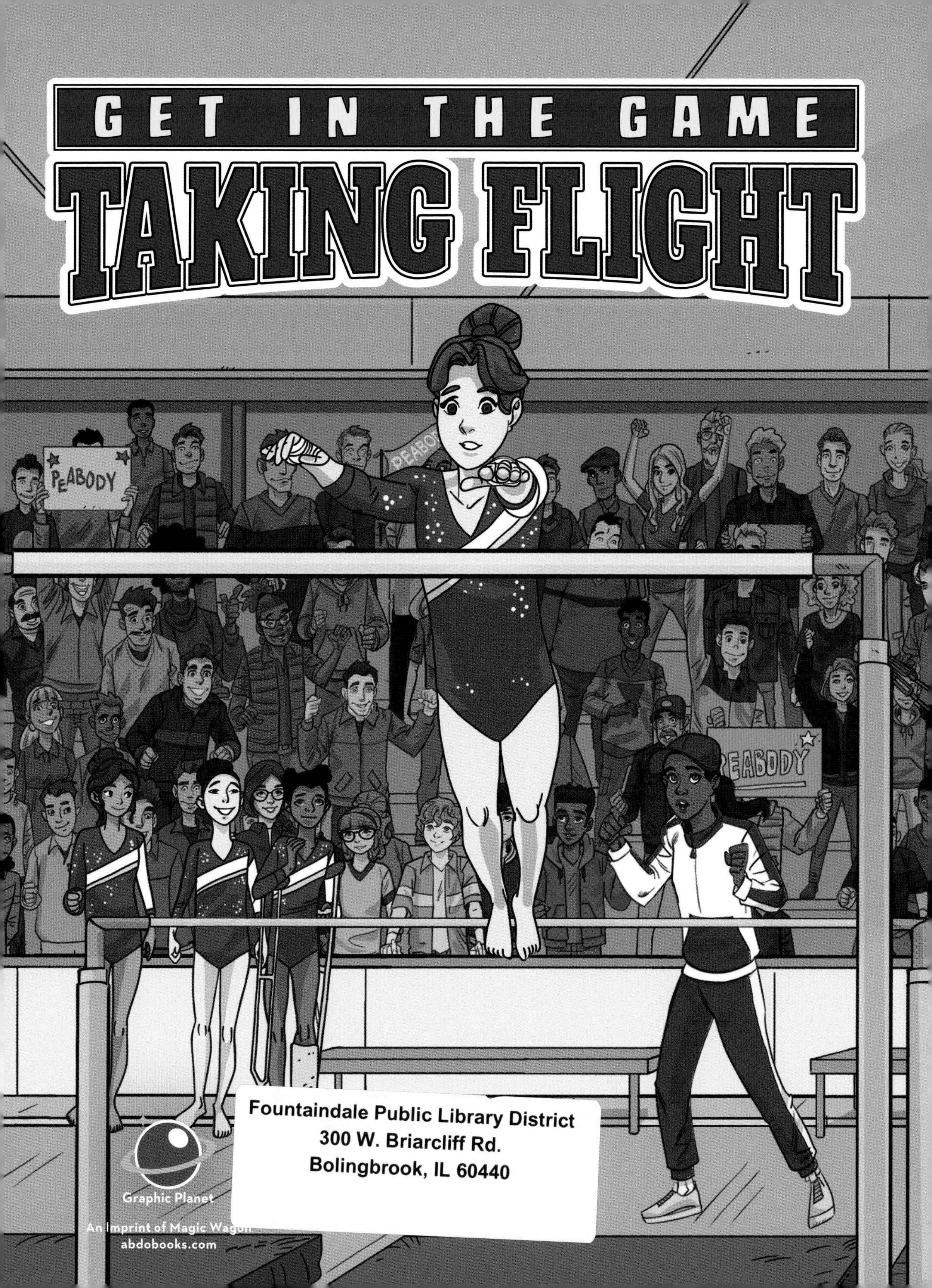
GET IN THE GAME
TAKING FLIGHT
PEABODY
PEABODY
PEABODY
Graphic Planet
An Imprint of Magic Wagon
abdobooks.com

abdobooks.com

Published by Magic Wagon, a division of ABDO, PO Box 398166, Minneapolis, Minnesota 55439.
Copyright © 2021 by Abdo Consulting Group, Inc. International copyrights reserved in all countries.
No part of this book may be reproduced in any form without written permission from the publisher.
Graphic Planet™ is a trademark and logo of Magic Wagon.

Printed in the United States of America, North Mankato, Minnesota.
082020
012021

Written by Bill Yu
Illustrated by Eduardo Garcia
Colored by Sebastian Garcia
Lettered by Kathryn S. Renta
Layout and design by Michelle Principe and Pejee Calanog of Glass House Graphics
    and Christina Doffing of ABDO
Editorial supervision by David Campiti
Packaged by Glass House Graphics
Art Directed by Candice Keimig and Laura Graphenteen
Editorial Support by Tamara L. Britton

Library of Congress Control Number: 2020930750

Publisher's Cataloging-in-Publication Data

Names: Yu, Bill, author. | Garcia, Eduardo; Garcia, Sebastian, illustrators.
Title: Taking flight / by Bill Yu ; illustrated by Eduardo Garcia and Sebastian Garcia.
Description: Minneapolis, Minnesota : Magic Wagon, 2021. | Series: Get in the game
Summary: Lucy Andia competes on Peabody's gymnastics team. She excels at floor exercise, but Coach
    Dawson moves her to uneven bars. Lucy is used to being on the floor. The high bar is more than eight
    feet off the ground! After numerous falls, Lucy is too scared to continue. Will Lucy quit the team?
    How can she overcome her fear of falling?
Identifiers: ISBN 9781532138331 (lib. bdg.) | ISBN 9781644944820 (pbk.) | ISBN 9781532139055
    (ebook) | ISBN 9781532139413 (Read-to-Me ebook)
Subjects: LCSH: Gymnastics--Juvenile fiction. | Sports teams--Juvenile fiction. | Floor exercise
    (Gymnastics)--Juvenile fiction. | Sports accidents--Juvenile fiction. | Fear--Juvenile fiction.
Classification: DDC [741.5]--dc23

CONTENTS

TAKING FLIGHT

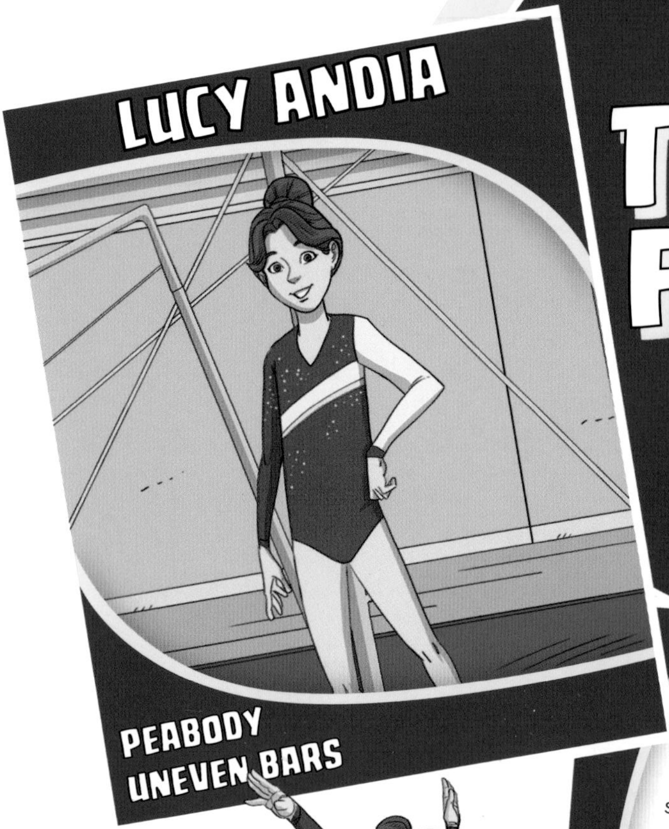
LUCY ANDIA
PEABODY
UNEVEN BARS

LUCY ANDIA,
Uneven Bars

Lucy Andia is coming off a gold medal season with a stellar performance in the floor exercise. She'll need to come up big on the uneven bars if Peabody is to advance to state again this season! Lucy's favorite gymnasts are Simone Biles and Laurie Hernandez.

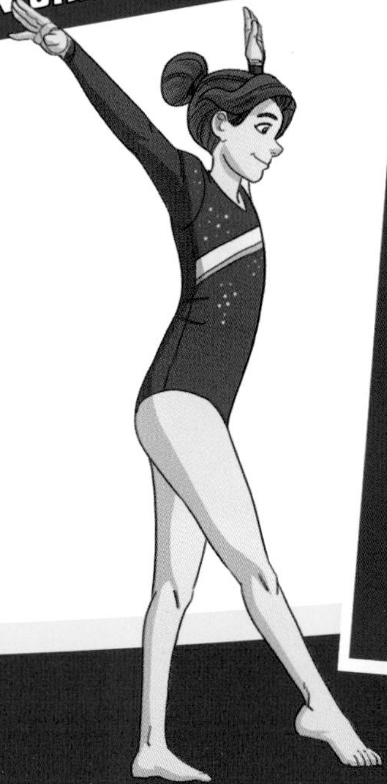

RECORD

	GOLD	SILVER	BRONZE
BALANCE BEAM	0	0	0
FLOOR EXERCISE	1	0	0
UNEVEN BARS	0	0	0
VAULT	0	0	0

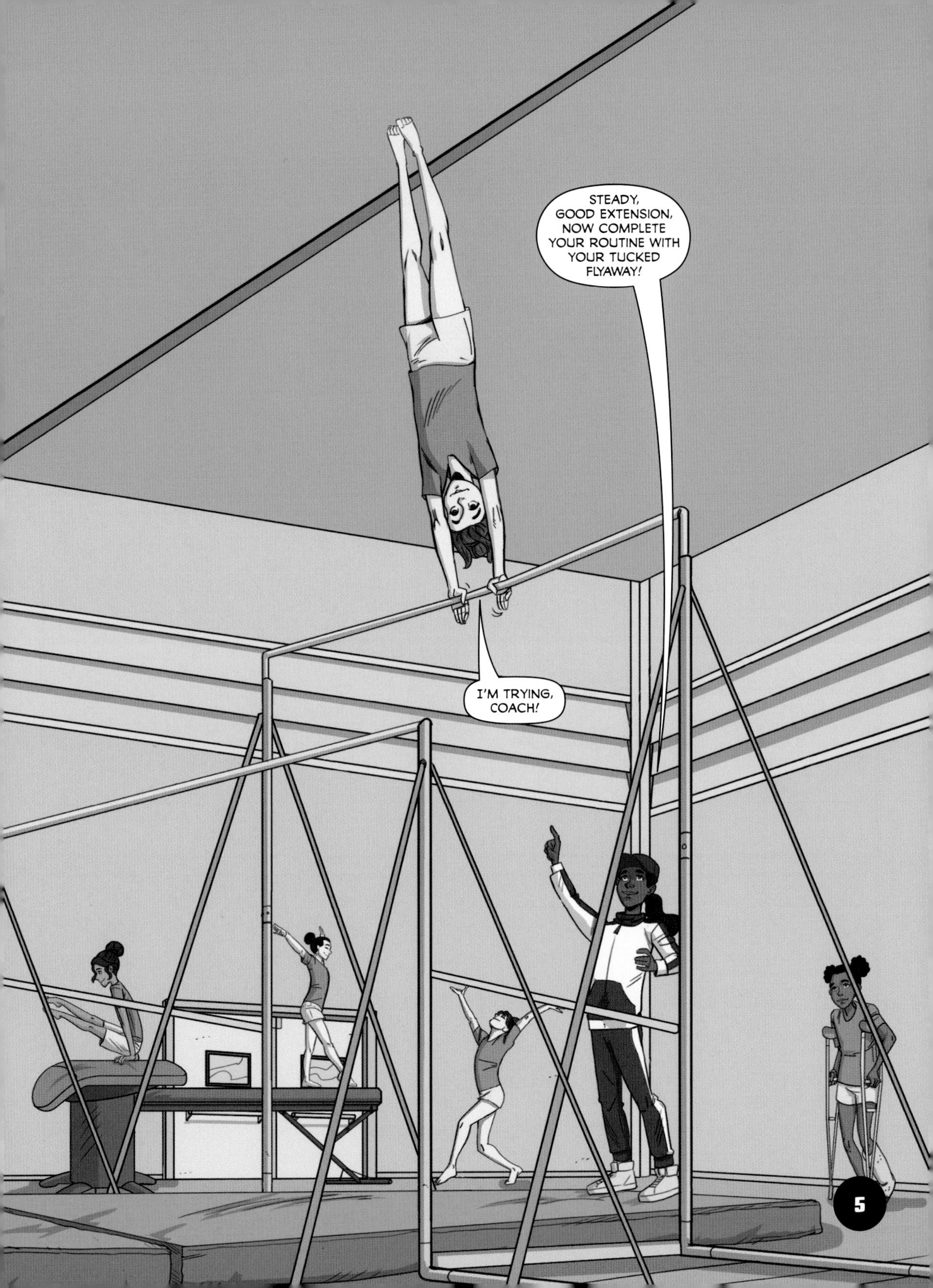
STEADY, GOOD EXTENSION, NOW COMPLETE YOUR ROUTINE WITH YOUR TUCKED FLYAWAY!
I'M TRYING, COACH!

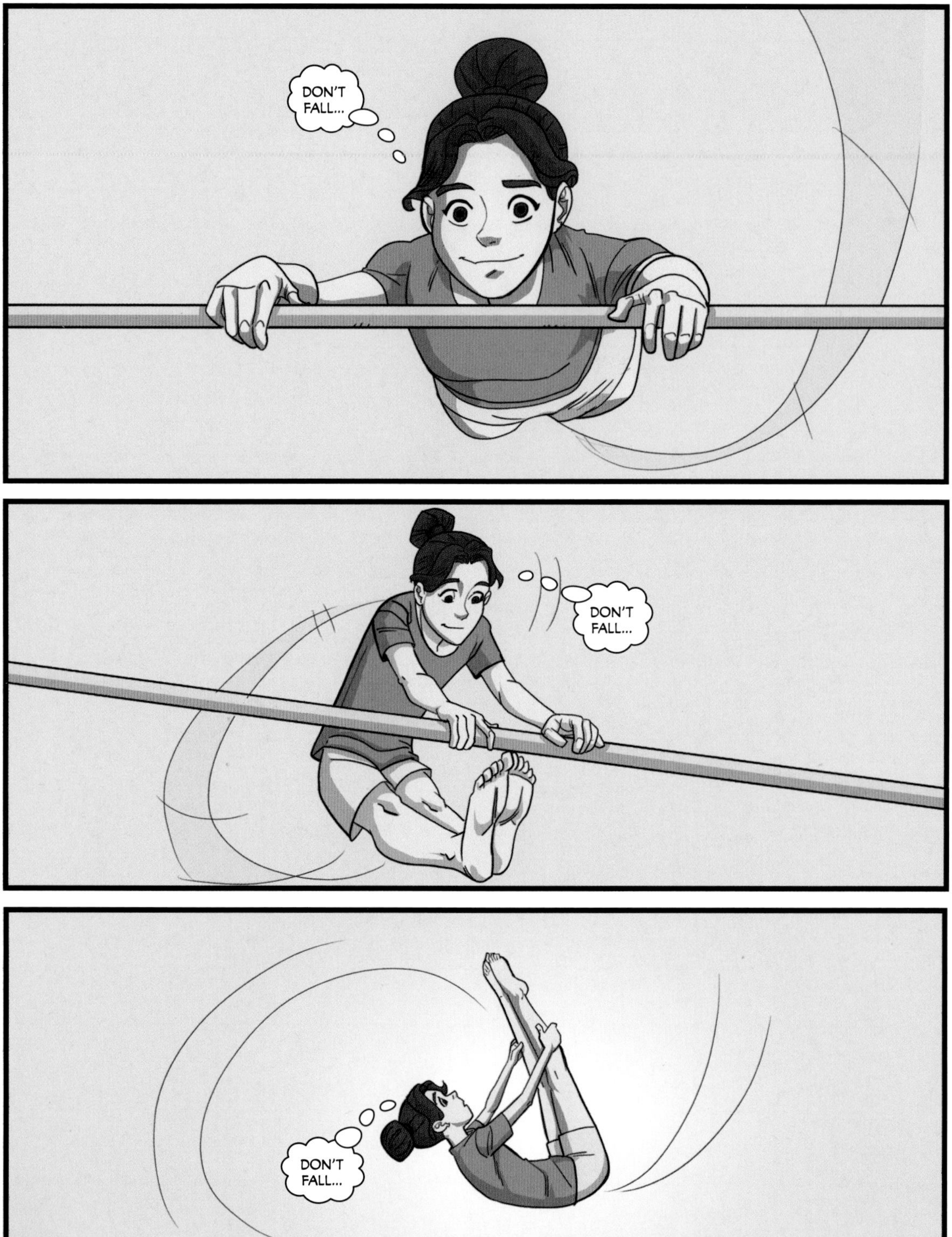
DON'T FALL...
DON'T FALL...
DON'T FALL...

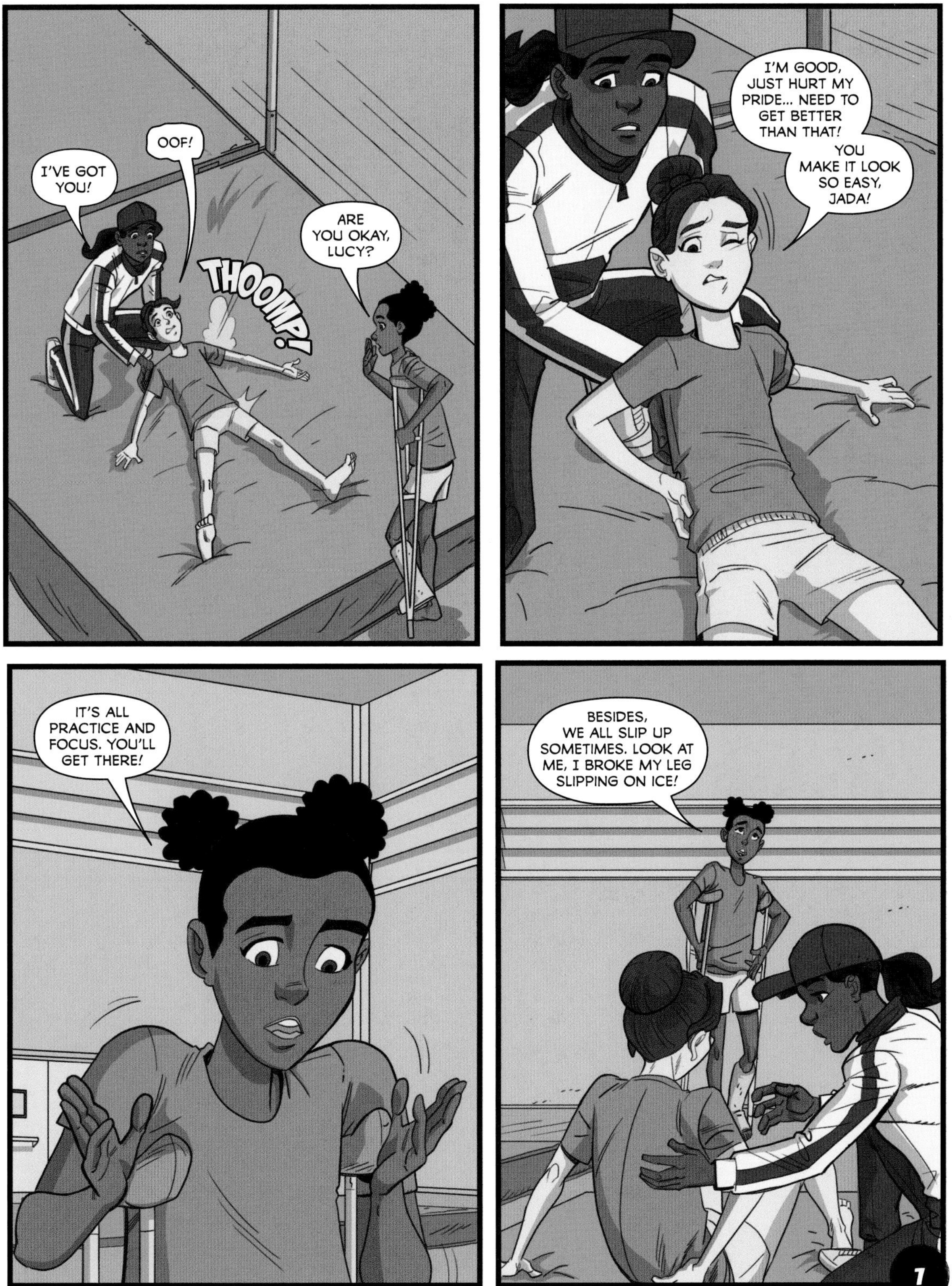
I'VE GOT YOU!
OOF!
THOOMP!
ARE YOU OKAY, LUCY?
I'M GOOD, JUST HURT MY PRIDE... NEED TO GET BETTER THAN THAT!
YOU MAKE IT LOOK SO EASY, JADA!
IT'S ALL PRACTICE AND FOCUS. YOU'LL GET THERE!
BESIDES, WE ALL SLIP UP SOMETIMES. LOOK AT ME, I BROKE MY LEG SLIPPING ON ICE!

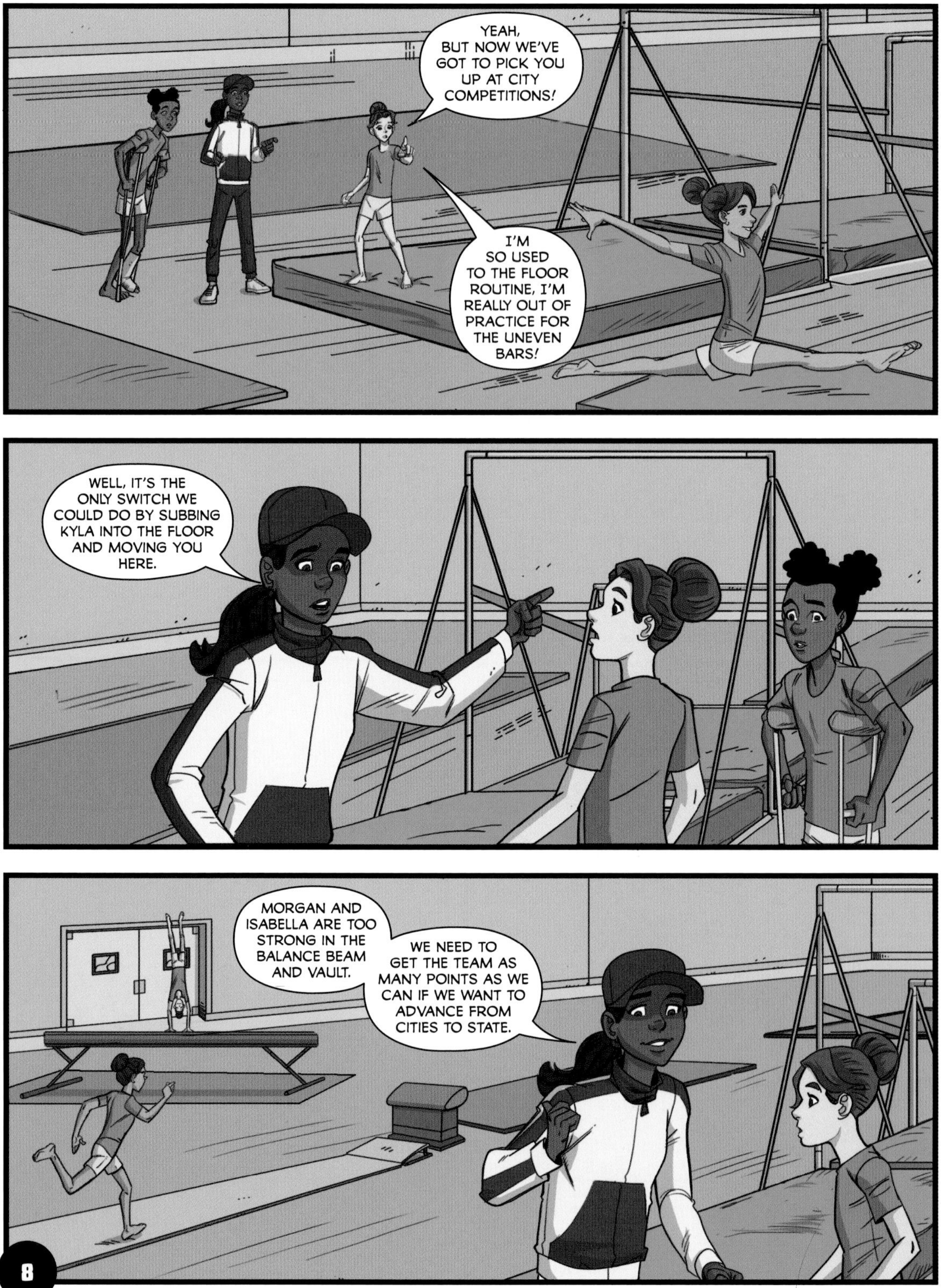
YEAH, BUT NOW WE'VE GOT TO PICK YOU UP AT CITY COMPETITIONS!
I'M SO USED TO THE FLOOR ROUTINE, I'M REALLY OUT OF PRACTICE FOR THE UNEVEN BARS!
WELL, IT'S THE ONLY SWITCH WE COULD DO BY SUBBING KYLA INTO THE FLOOR AND MOVING YOU HERE.
MORGAN AND ISABELLA ARE TOO STRONG IN THE BALANCE BEAM AND VAULT.
WE NEED TO GET THE TEAM AS MANY POINTS AS WE CAN IF WE WANT TO ADVANCE FROM CITIES TO STATE.

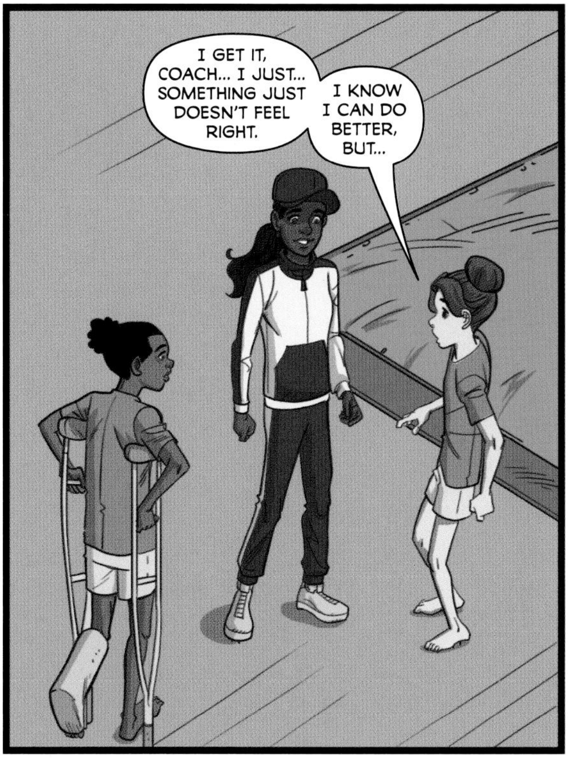
I GET IT, COACH... I JUST... SOMETHING JUST DOESN'T FEEL RIGHT.
I KNOW I CAN DO BETTER, BUT...

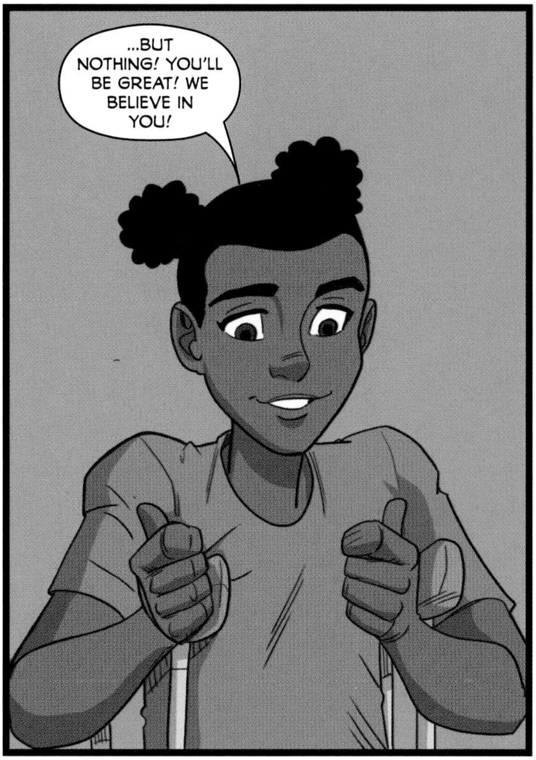
...BUT NOTHING! YOU'LL BE GREAT! WE BELIEVE IN YOU!

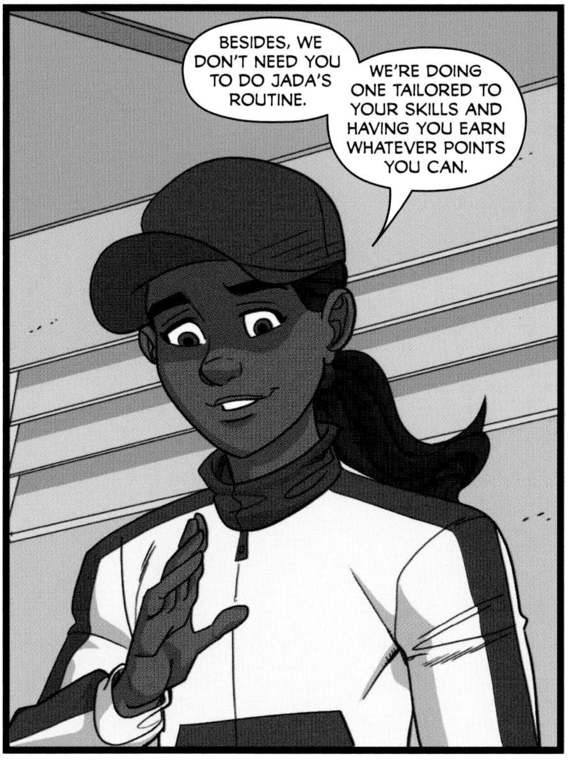
BESIDES, WE DON'T NEED YOU TO DO JADA'S ROUTINE.
WE'RE DOING ONE TAILORED TO YOUR SKILLS AND HAVING YOU EARN WHATEVER POINTS YOU CAN.

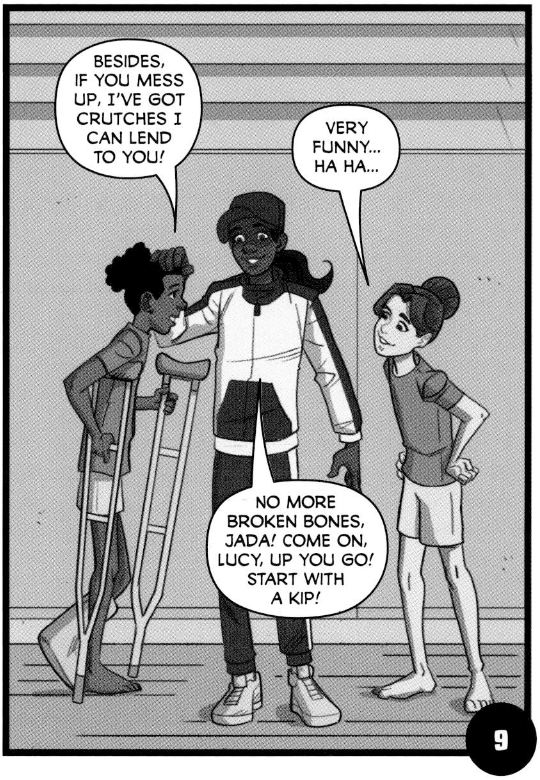
BESIDES, IF YOU MESS UP, I'VE GOT CRUTCHES I CAN LEND TO YOU!
VERY FUNNY... HA HA...
NO MORE BROKEN BONES, JADA! COME ON, LUCY, UP YOU GO! START WITH A KIP!

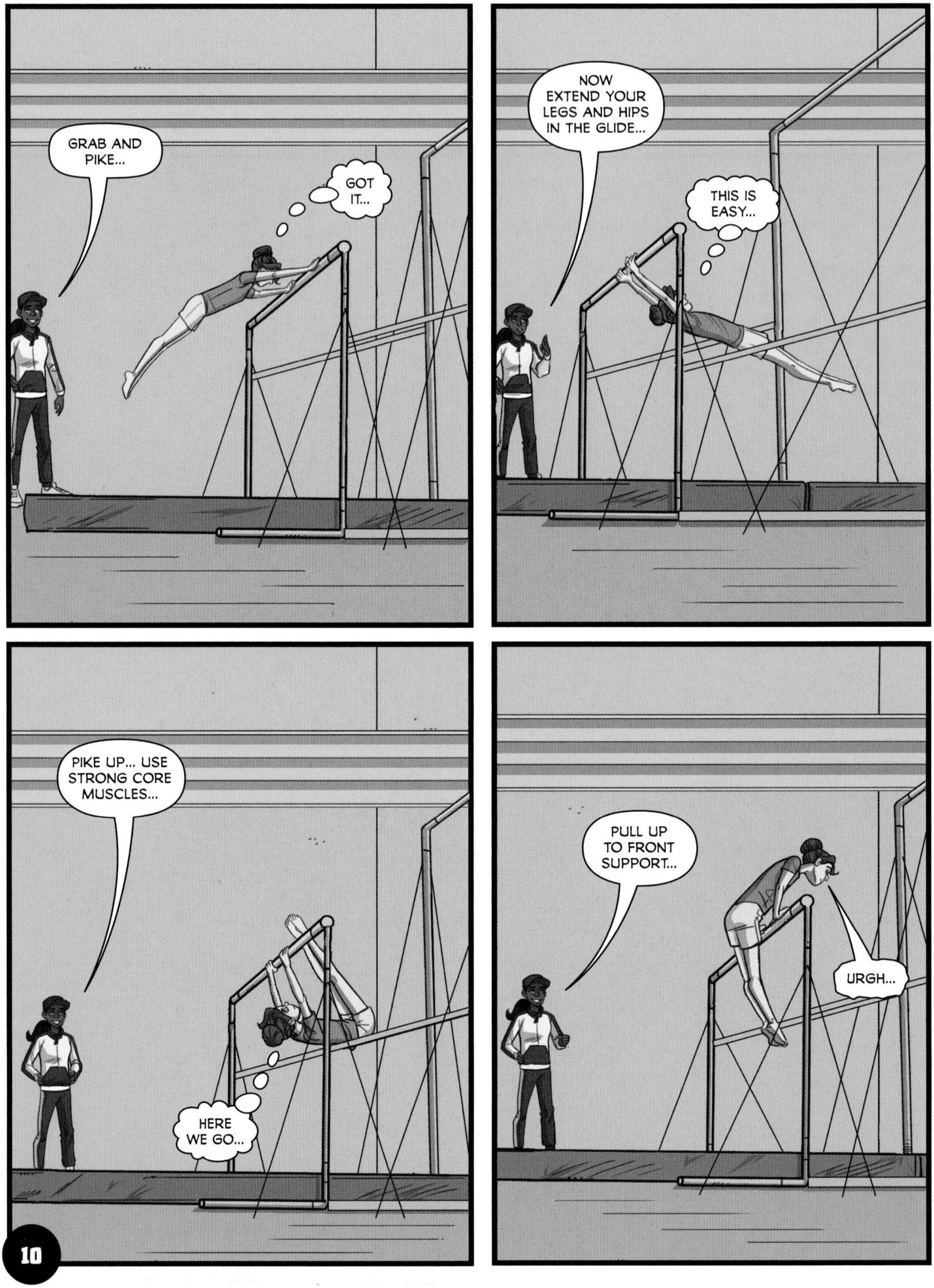
GRAB AND PIKE...
GOT IT...
NOW EXTEND YOUR LEGS AND HIPS IN THE GLIDE...
THIS IS EASY...
PIKE UP... USE STRONG CORE MUSCLES...
HERE WE GO...
PULL UP TO FRONT SUPPORT...
URGH...

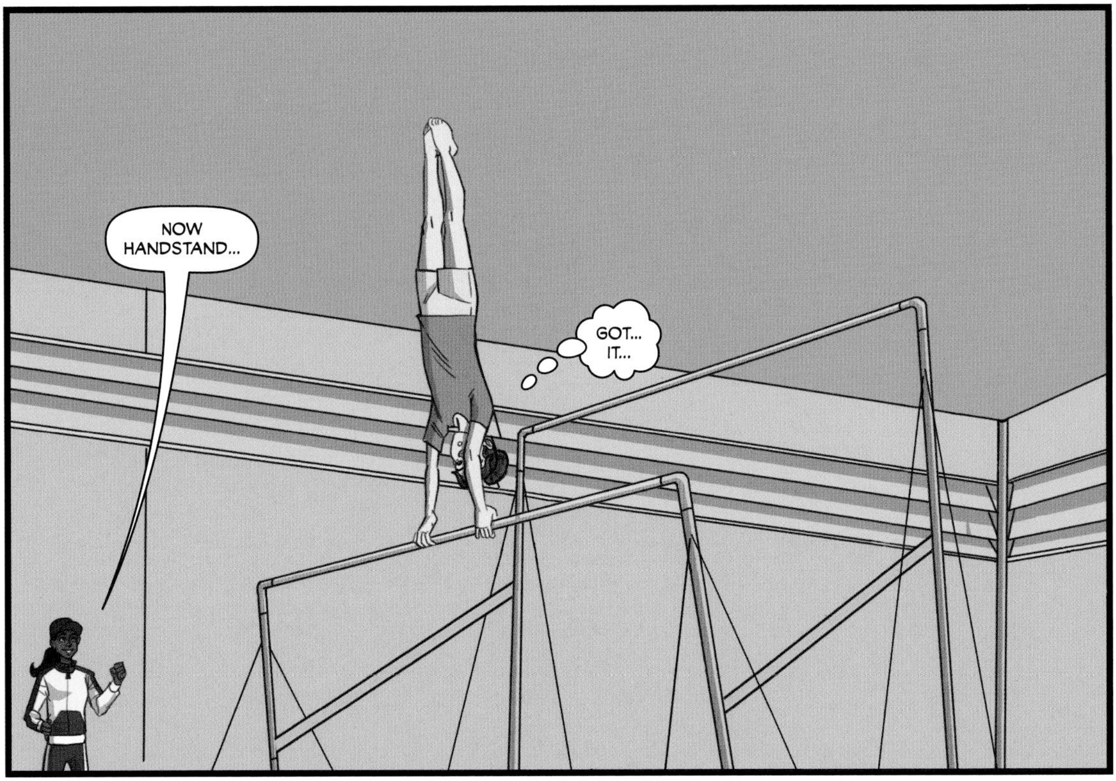
NOW HANDSTAND...
GOT... IT...

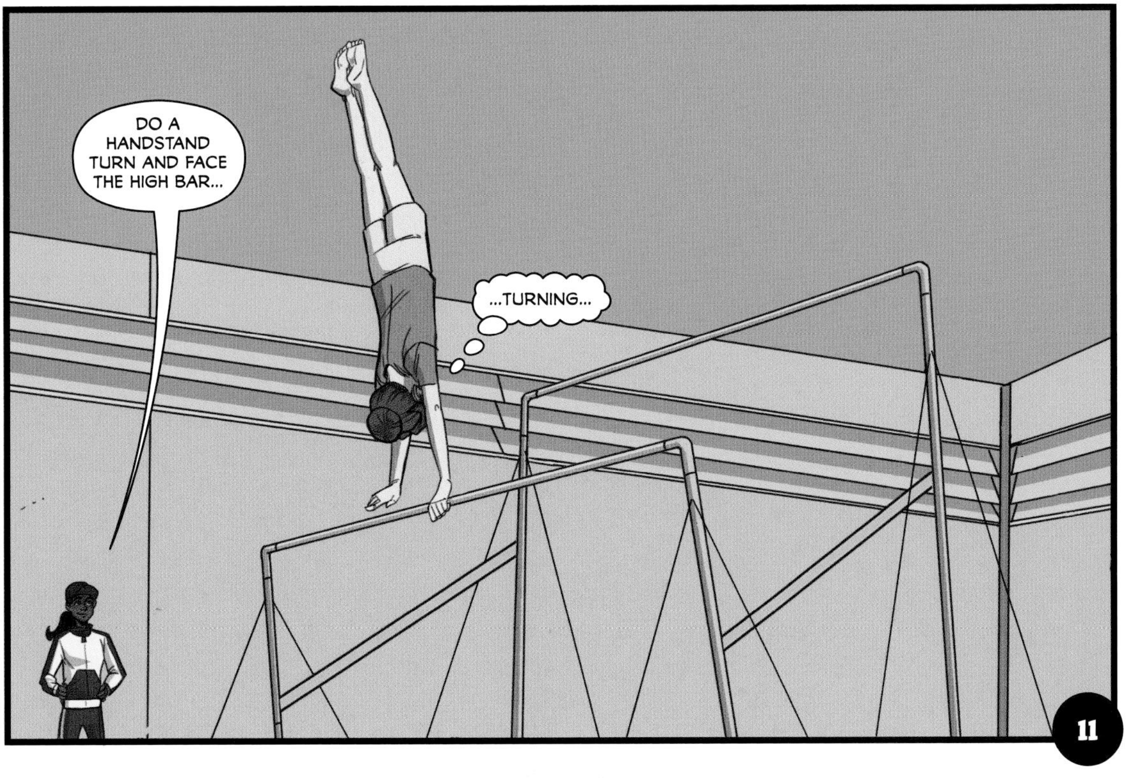
DO A HANDSTAND TURN AND FACE THE HIGH BAR...
...TURNING...

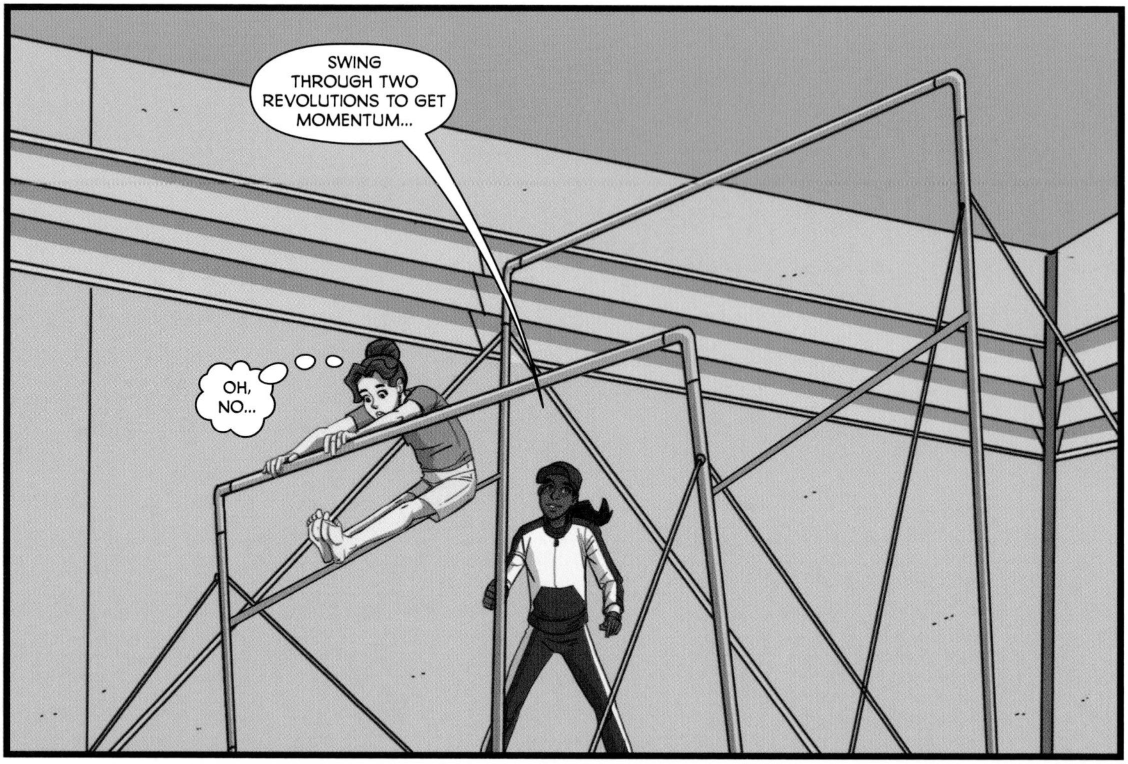
SWING THROUGH TWO REVOLUTIONS TO GET MOMENTUM...
OH, NO...

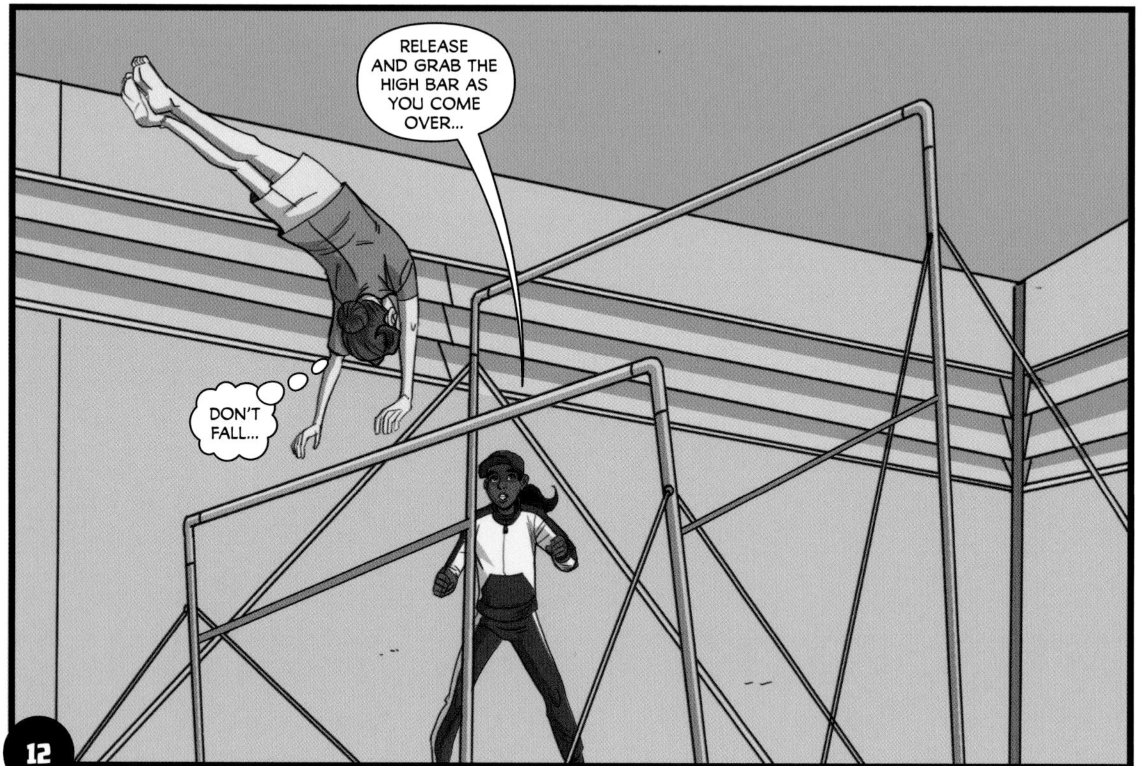
RELEASE AND GRAB THE HIGH BAR AS YOU COME OVER...
DON'T FALL...

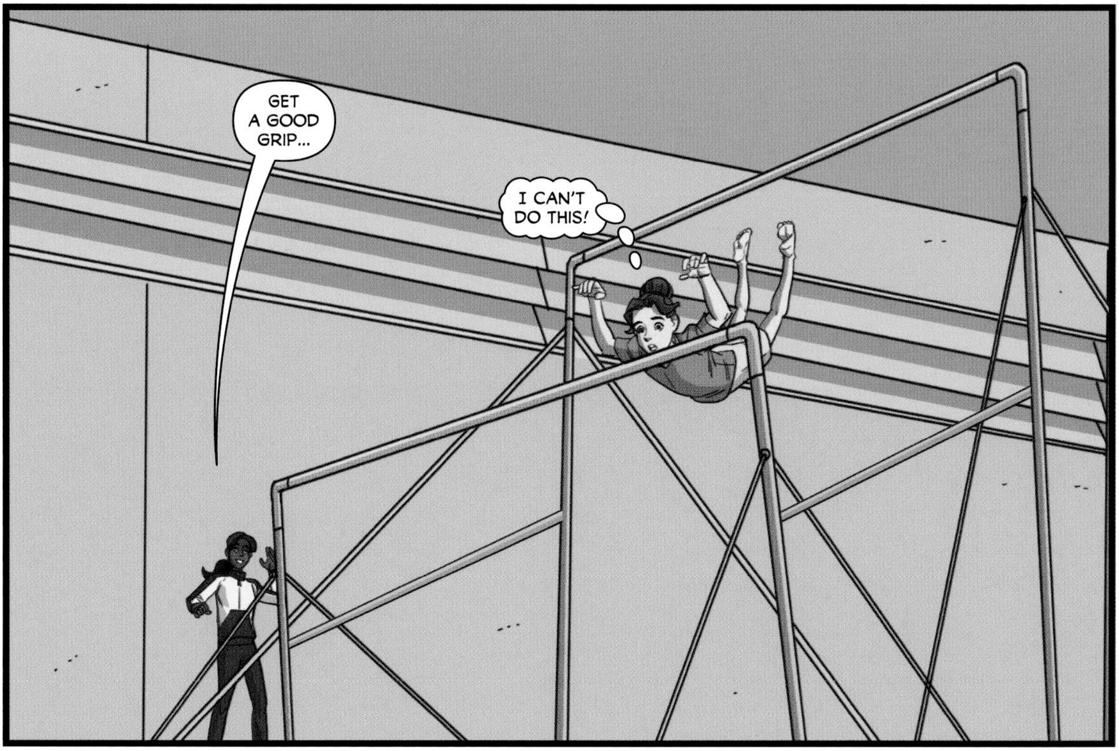
GET A GOOD GRIP...
I CAN'T DO THIS!

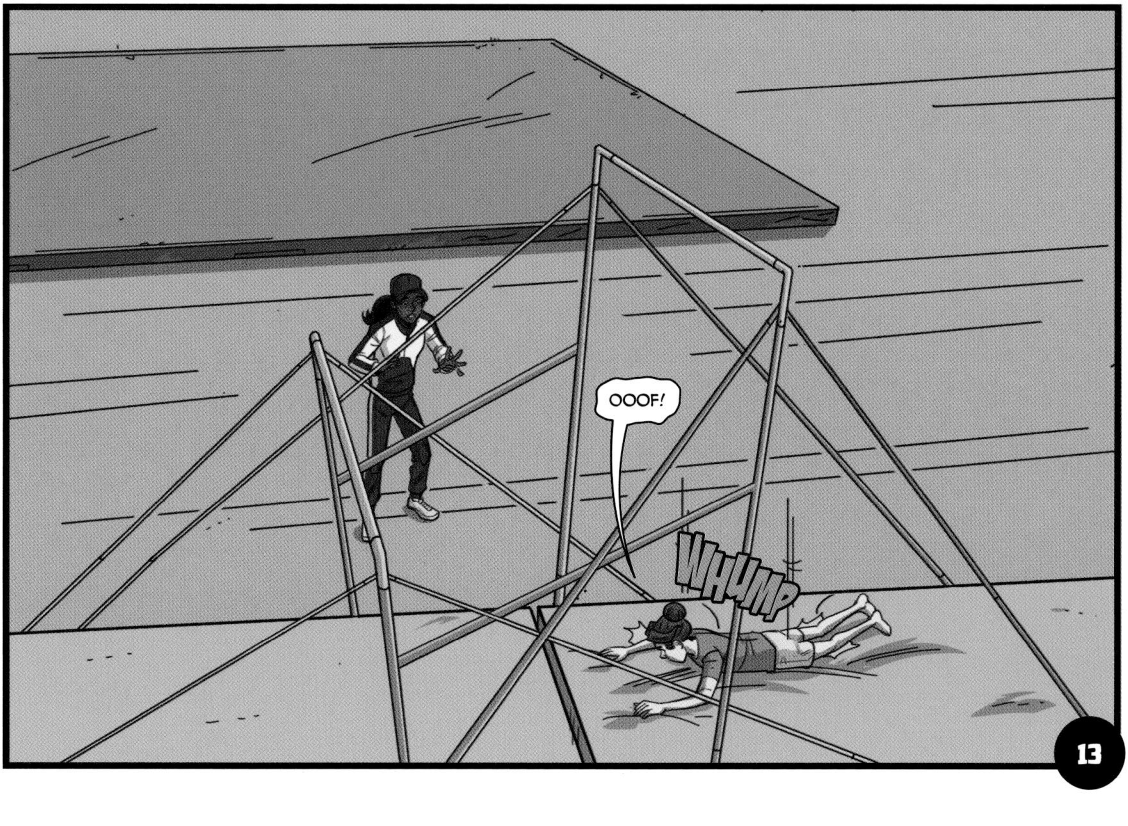
OOOF!
WHUMP

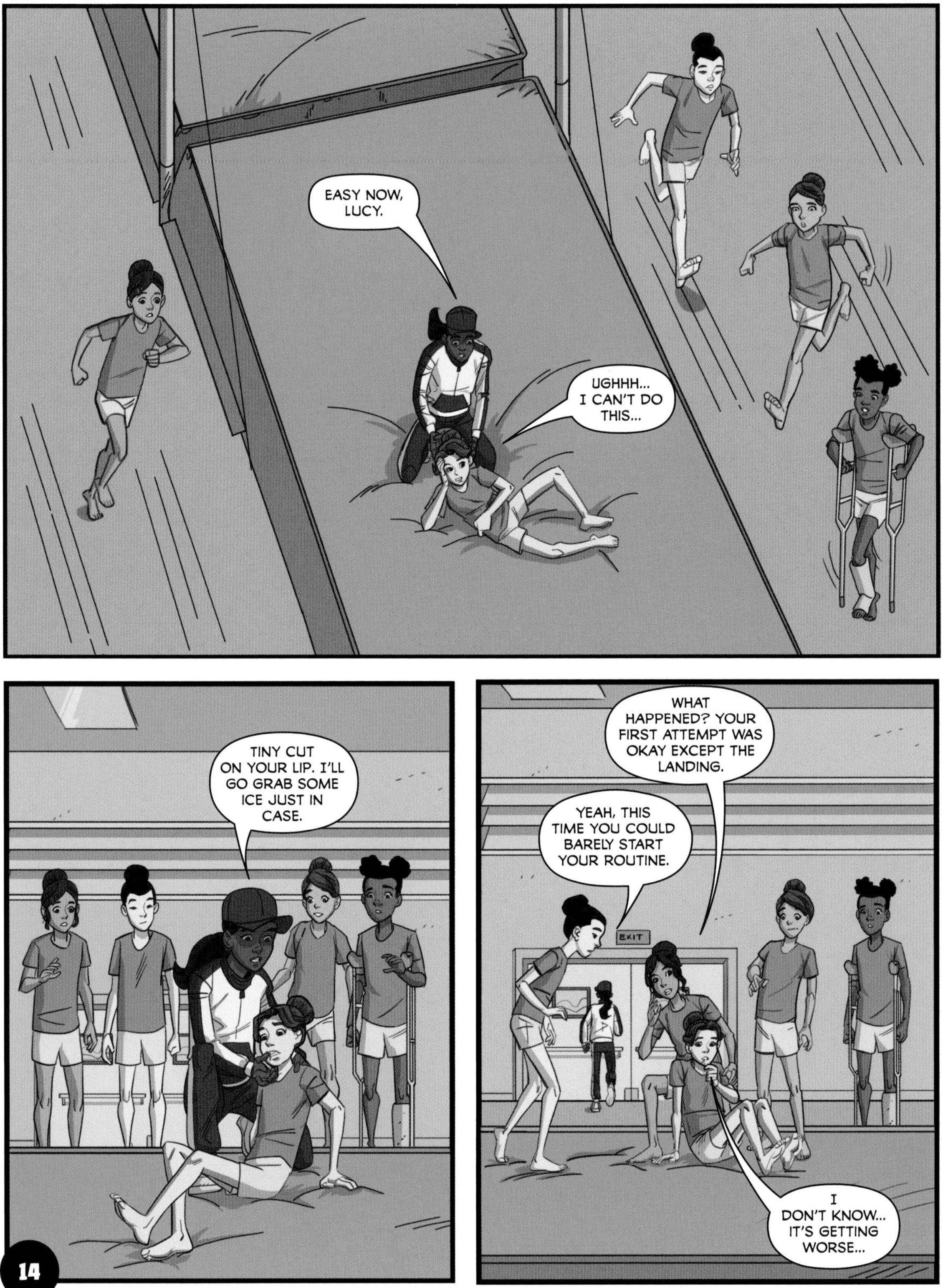
EASY NOW, LUCY.
UGHHH... I CAN'T DO THIS...
TINY CUT ON YOUR LIP. I'LL GO GRAB SOME ICE JUST IN CASE.
WHAT HAPPENED? YOUR FIRST ATTEMPT WAS OKAY EXCEPT THE LANDING.
YEAH, THIS TIME YOU COULD BARELY START YOUR ROUTINE.
EXIT
I DON'T KNOW... IT'S GETTING WORSE...

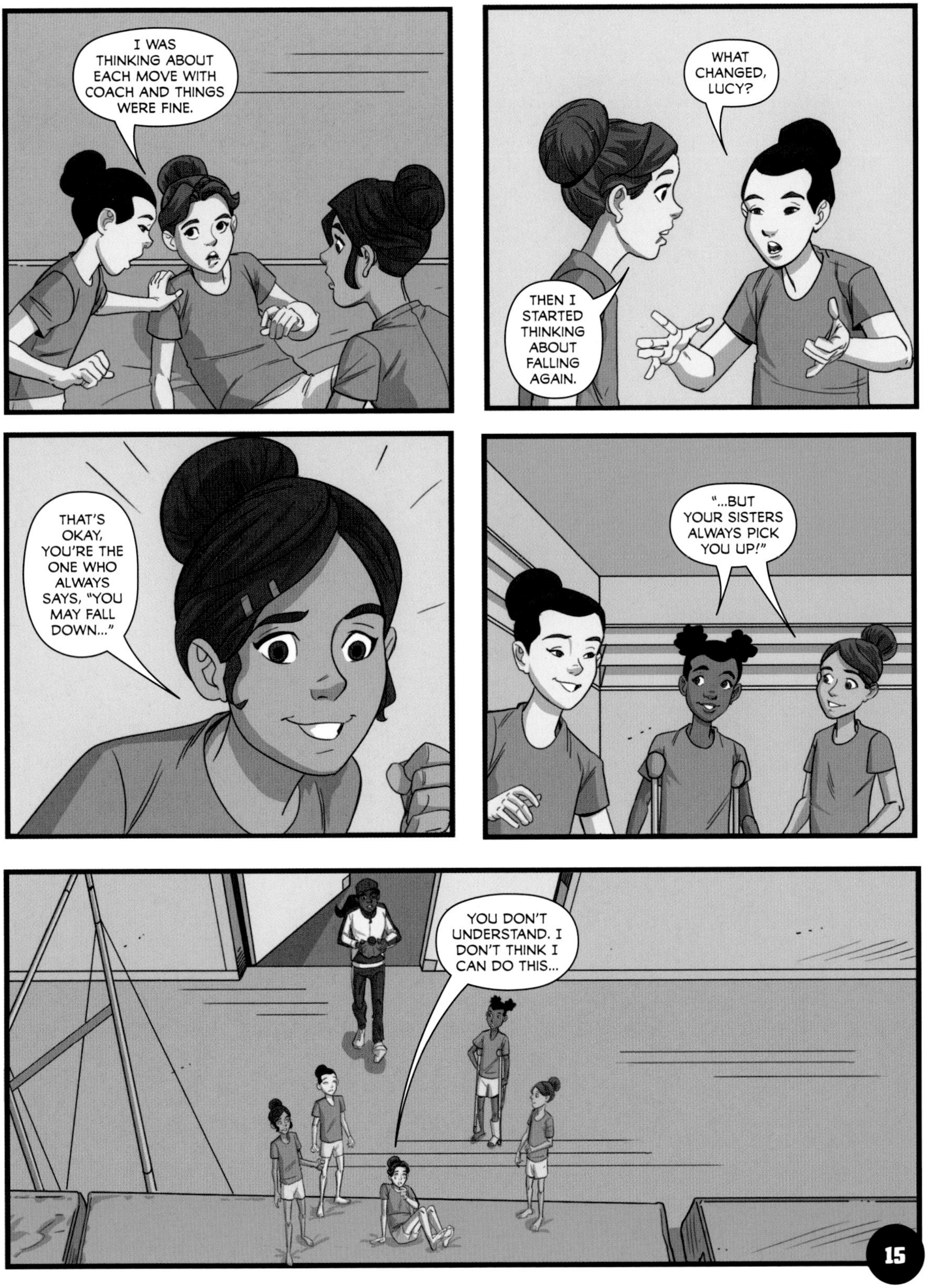
I WAS THINKING ABOUT EACH MOVE WITH COACH AND THINGS WERE FINE.
WHAT CHANGED, LUCY?
THEN I STARTED THINKING ABOUT FALLING AGAIN.
THAT'S OKAY, YOU'RE THE ONE WHO ALWAYS SAYS, "YOU MAY FALL DOWN..."
"...BUT YOUR SISTERS ALWAYS PICK YOU UP!"
YOU DON'T UNDERSTAND. I DON'T THINK I CAN DO THIS...

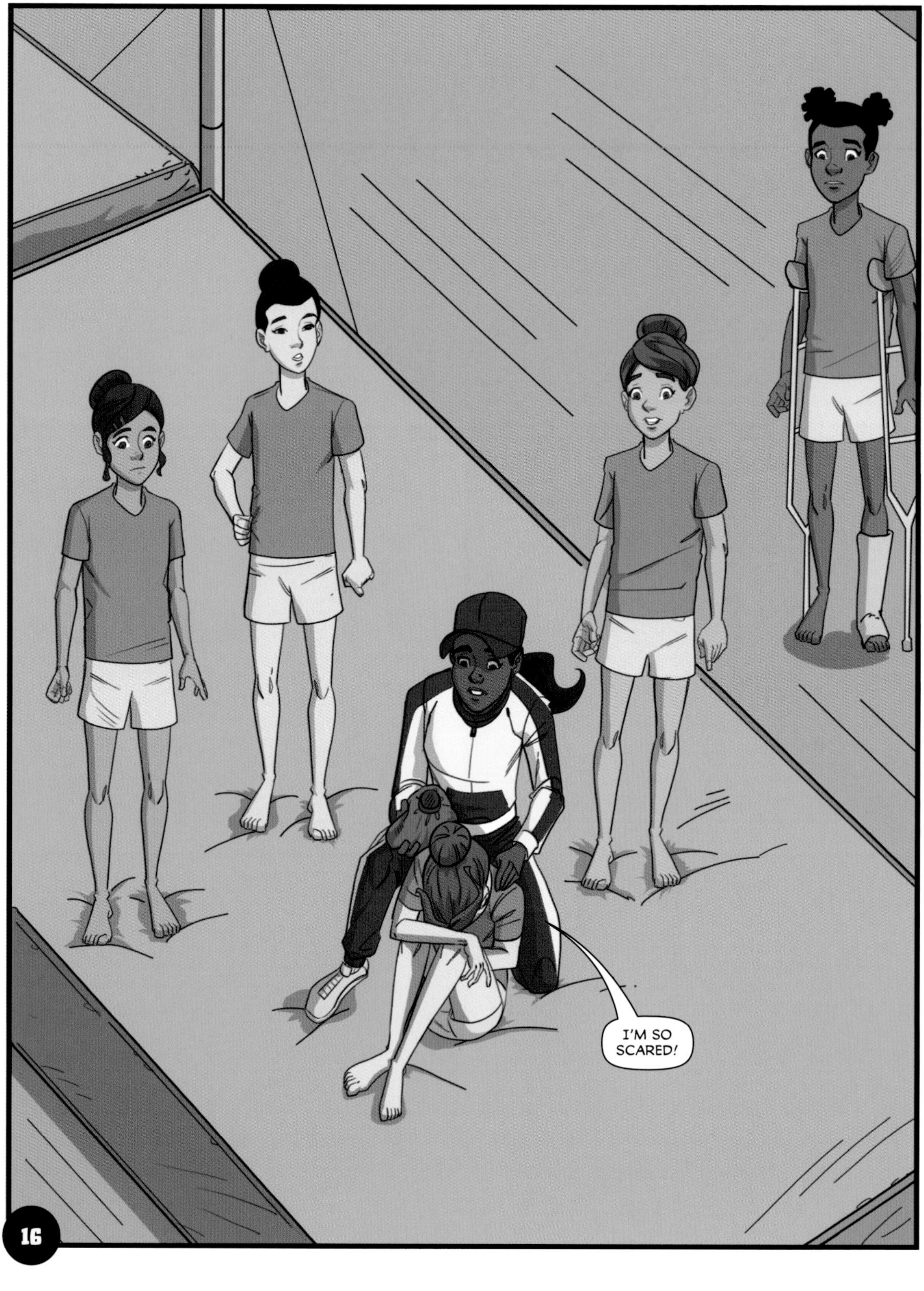
I'M SO SCARED!

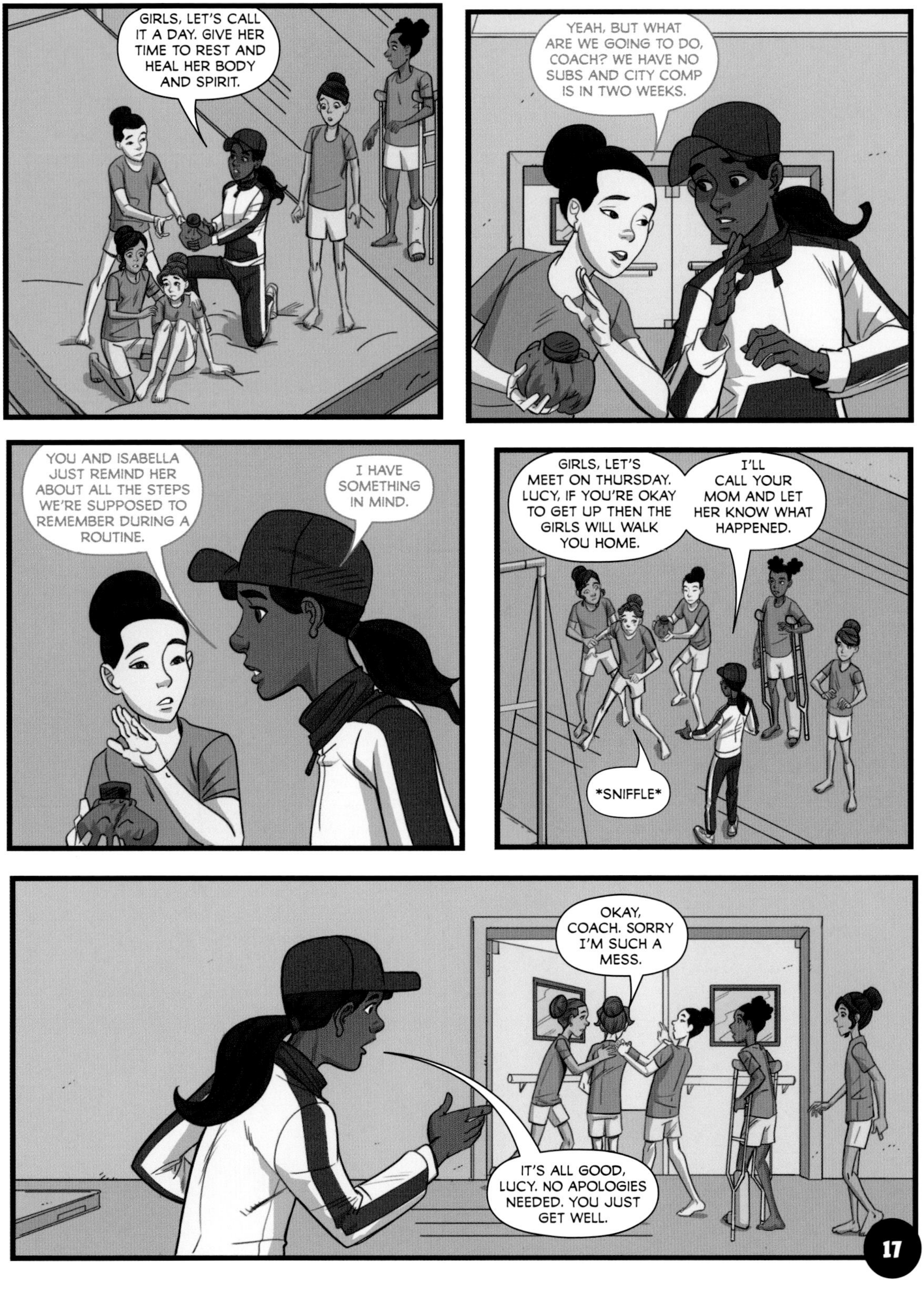
GIRLS, LET'S CALL IT A DAY. GIVE HER TIME TO REST AND HEAL HER BODY AND SPIRIT.
YEAH, BUT WHAT ARE WE GOING TO DO, COACH? WE HAVE NO SUBS AND CITY COMP IS IN TWO WEEKS.
YOU AND ISABELLA JUST REMIND HER ABOUT ALL THE STEPS WE'RE SUPPOSED TO REMEMBER DURING A ROUTINE.
I HAVE SOMETHING IN MIND.
GIRLS, LET'S MEET ON THURSDAY. LUCY, IF YOU'RE OKAY TO GET UP THEN THE GIRLS WILL WALK YOU HOME.
I'LL CALL YOUR MOM AND LET HER KNOW WHAT HAPPENED.
SNIFFLE
OKAY, COACH. SORRY I'M SUCH A MESS.
IT'S ALL GOOD, LUCY. NO APOLOGIES NEEDED. YOU JUST GET WELL.

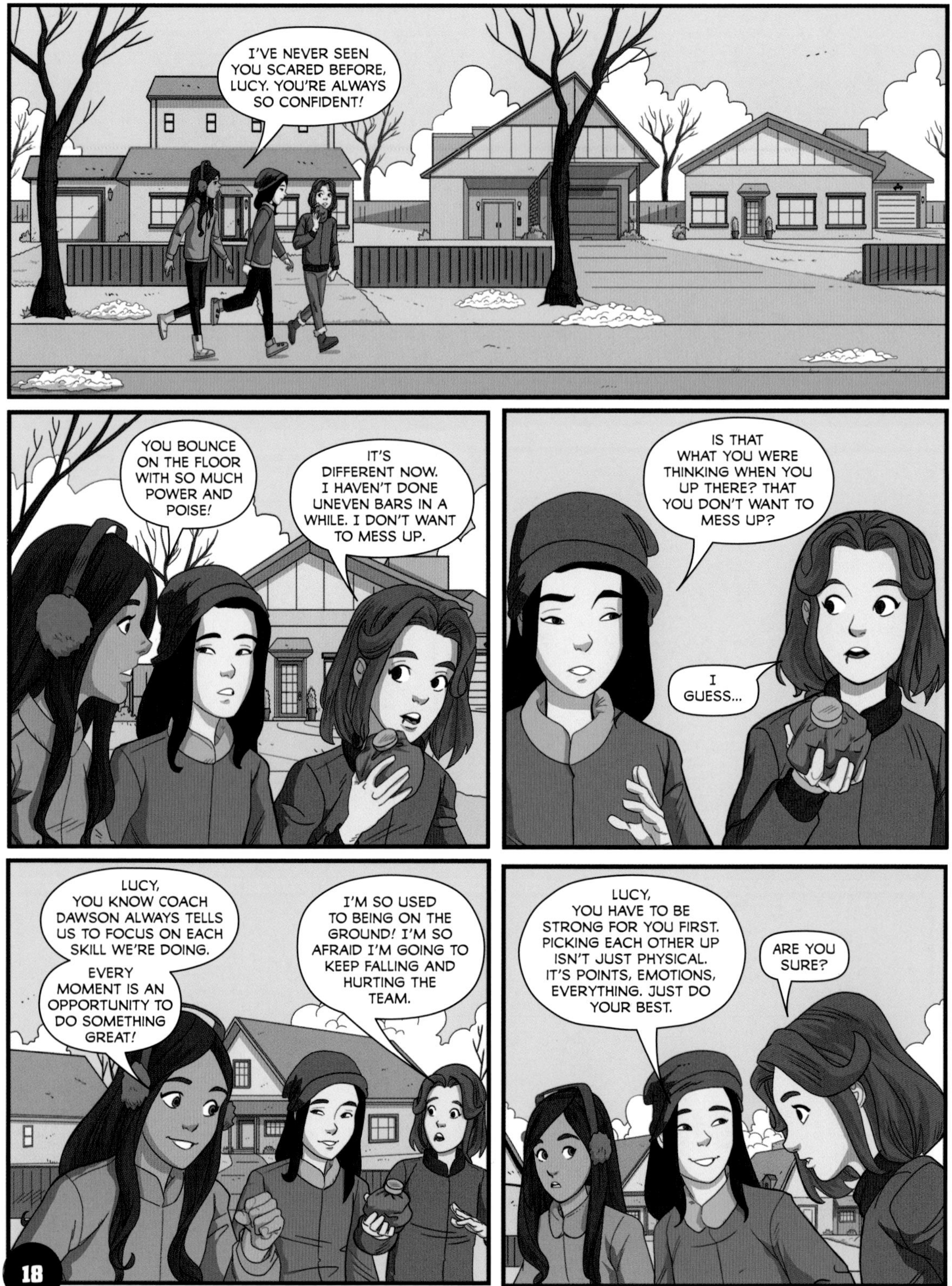
I'VE NEVER SEEN YOU SCARED BEFORE, LUCY. YOU'RE ALWAYS SO CONFIDENT!
YOU BOUNCE ON THE FLOOR WITH SO MUCH POWER AND POISE!
IT'S DIFFERENT NOW. I HAVEN'T DONE UNEVEN BARS IN A WHILE. I DON'T WANT TO MESS UP.
IS THAT WHAT YOU WERE THINKING WHEN YOU UP THERE? THAT YOU DON'T WANT TO MESS UP?
I GUESS...
LUCY, YOU KNOW COACH DAWSON ALWAYS TELLS US TO FOCUS ON EACH SKILL WE'RE DOING.
EVERY MOMENT IS AN OPPORTUNITY TO DO SOMETHING GREAT!
I'M SO USED TO BEING ON THE GROUND! I'M SO AFRAID I'M GOING TO KEEP FALLING AND HURTING THE TEAM.
LUCY, YOU HAVE TO BE STRONG FOR YOU FIRST. PICKING EACH OTHER UP ISN'T JUST PHYSICAL. IT'S POINTS, EMOTIONS, EVERYTHING. JUST DO YOUR BEST.
ARE YOU SURE?

MORGAN'S RIGHT. IF WE HAVE TO WORK HARDER TO GET MORE POINTS, WE'LL DO IT.

WE'LL PICK YOU UP AS A TEAM.

THANKS *MI HERMANA MAYOR DE GIMNASIA.*

NO PROBLEM, "MY LITTLE GYMNASTICS SISTER".

COACH DAWSON CALLED AND TOLD ME WHAT HAPPENED. YOU OKAY, LUCY?

I'M OKAY, JUST A SMALL CUT LIP.

I DIDN'T MEAN THE CUT, BUT I'M GLAD THAT'S OKAY TOO.

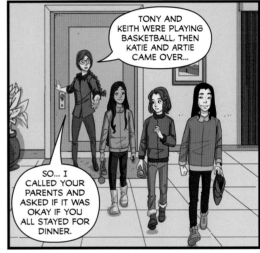

TONY AND KEITH WERE PLAYING BASKETBALL, THEN KATIE AND ARTIE CAME OVER...

SO... I CALLED YOUR PARENTS AND ASKED IF IT WAS OKAY IF YOU ALL STAYED FOR DINNER.

I FIGURED YOU COULD USE SOME CHEERING UP WITH YOUR FRIENDS AND SOME OF MY WORLD-FAMOUS SPAGHETTI!

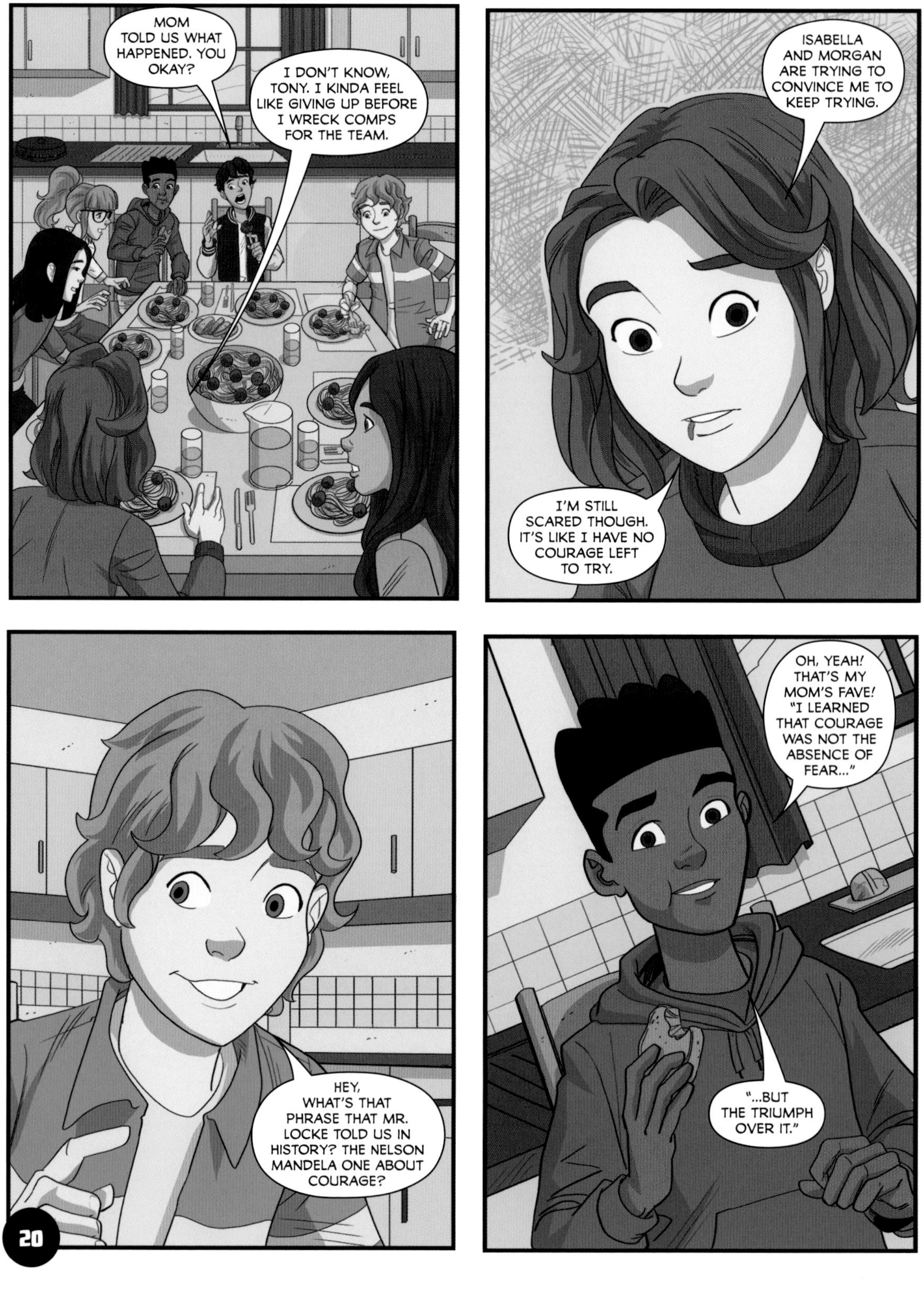
MOM TOLD US WHAT HAPPENED. YOU OKAY?
I DON'T KNOW, TONY. I KINDA FEEL LIKE GIVING UP BEFORE I WRECK COMPS FOR THE TEAM.
ISABELLA AND MORGAN ARE TRYING TO CONVINCE ME TO KEEP TRYING.
I'M STILL SCARED THOUGH. IT'S LIKE I HAVE NO COURAGE LEFT TO TRY.
HEY, WHAT'S THAT PHRASE THAT MR. LOCKE TOLD US IN HISTORY? THE NELSON MANDELA ONE ABOUT COURAGE?
OH, YEAH! THAT'S MY MOM'S FAVE! "I LEARNED THAT COURAGE WAS NOT THE ABSENCE OF FEAR..."
"...BUT THE TRIUMPH OVER IT."

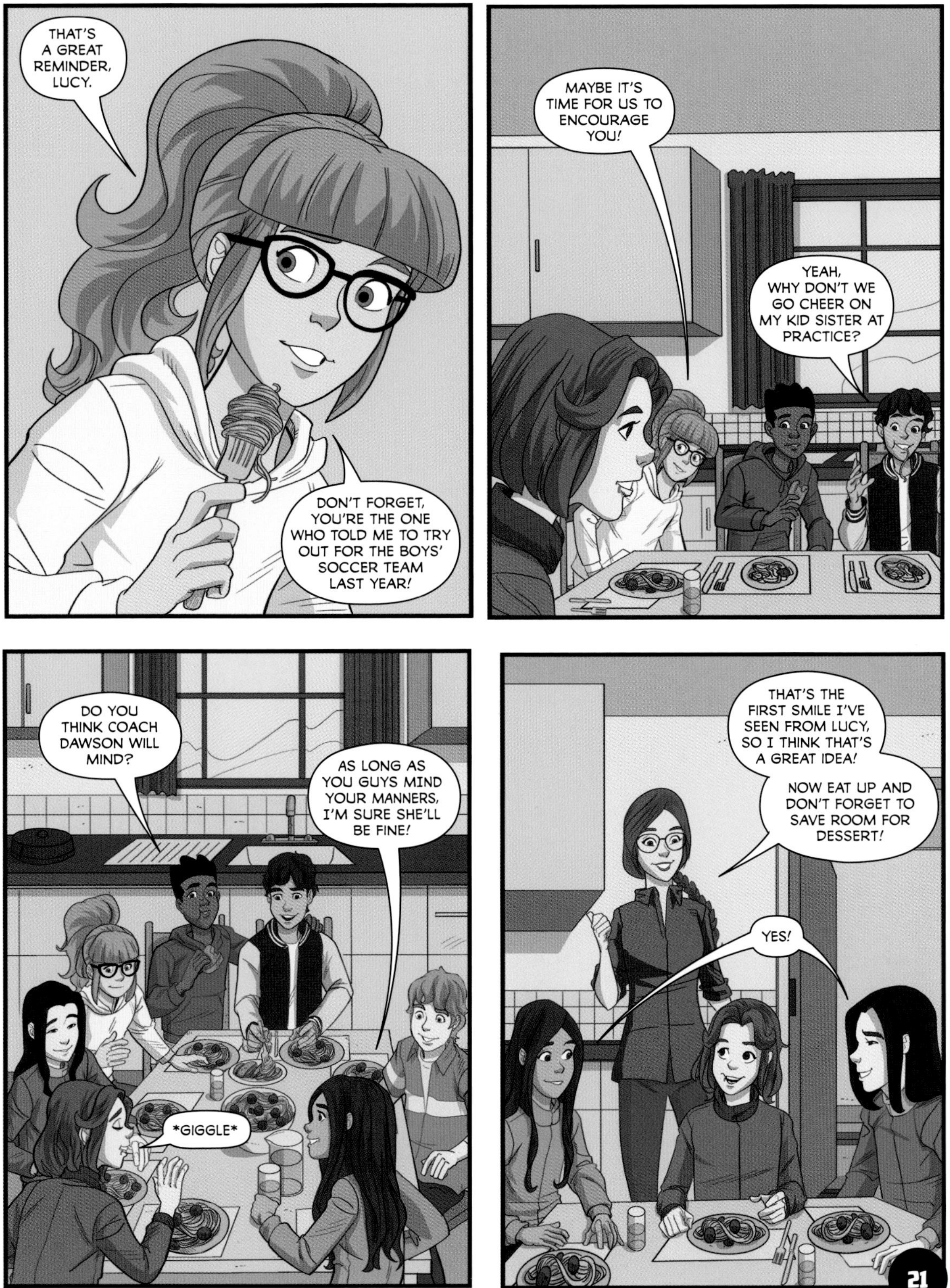
THAT'S A GREAT REMINDER, LUCY.
DON'T FORGET, YOU'RE THE ONE WHO TOLD ME TO TRY OUT FOR THE BOYS' SOCCER TEAM LAST YEAR!
MAYBE IT'S TIME FOR US TO ENCOURAGE YOU!
YEAH, WHY DON'T WE GO CHEER ON MY KID SISTER AT PRACTICE?
DO YOU THINK COACH DAWSON WILL MIND?
AS LONG AS YOU GUYS MIND YOUR MANNERS, I'M SURE SHE'LL BE FINE!
GIGGLE
THAT'S THE FIRST SMILE I'VE SEEN FROM LUCY, SO I THINK THAT'S A GREAT IDEA!
NOW EAT UP AND DON'T FORGET TO SAVE ROOM FOR DESSERT!
YES!

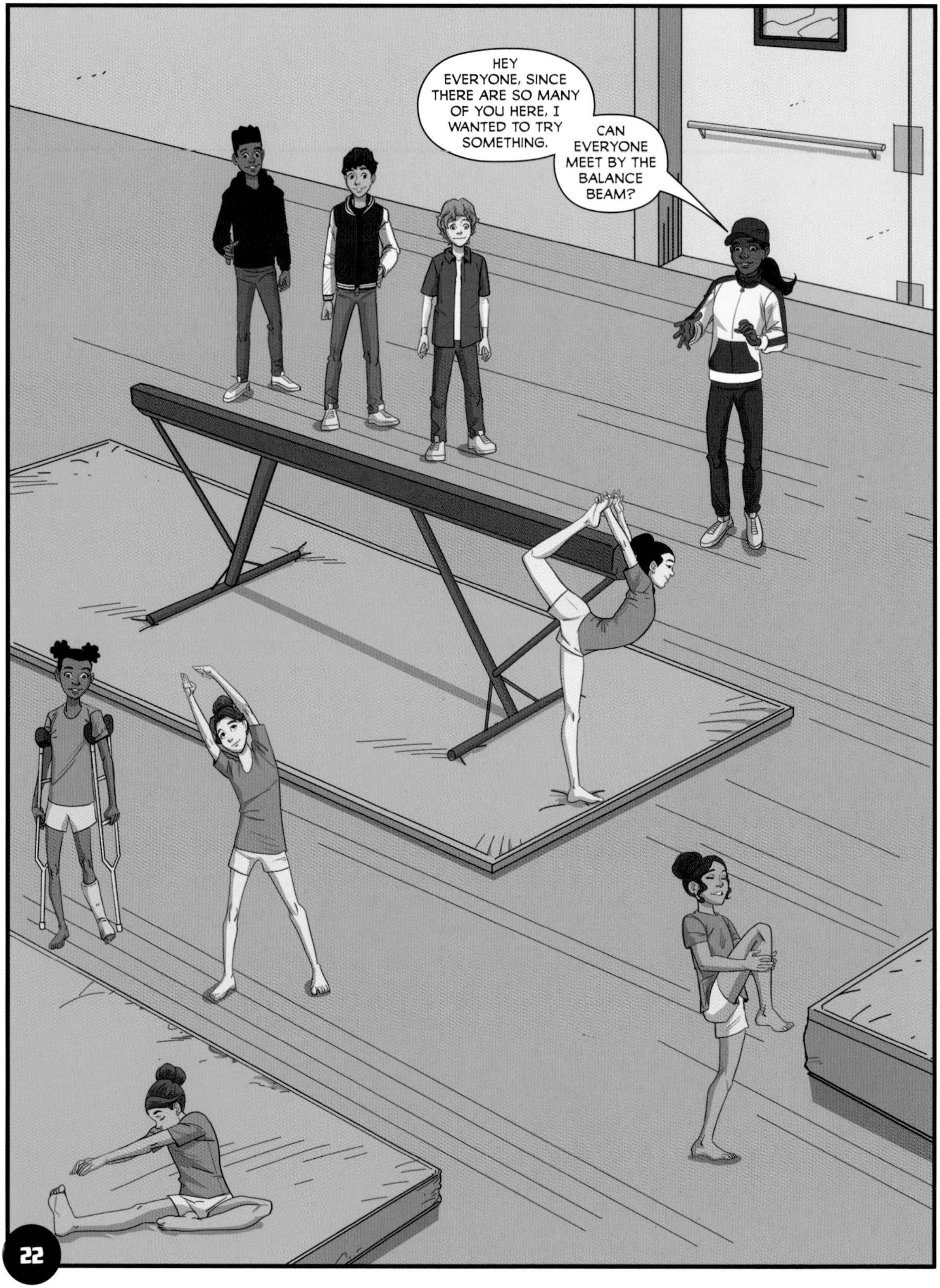
HEY EVERYONE, SINCE THERE ARE SO MANY OF YOU HERE, I WANTED TO TRY SOMETHING.
CAN EVERYONE MEET BY THE BALANCE BEAM?

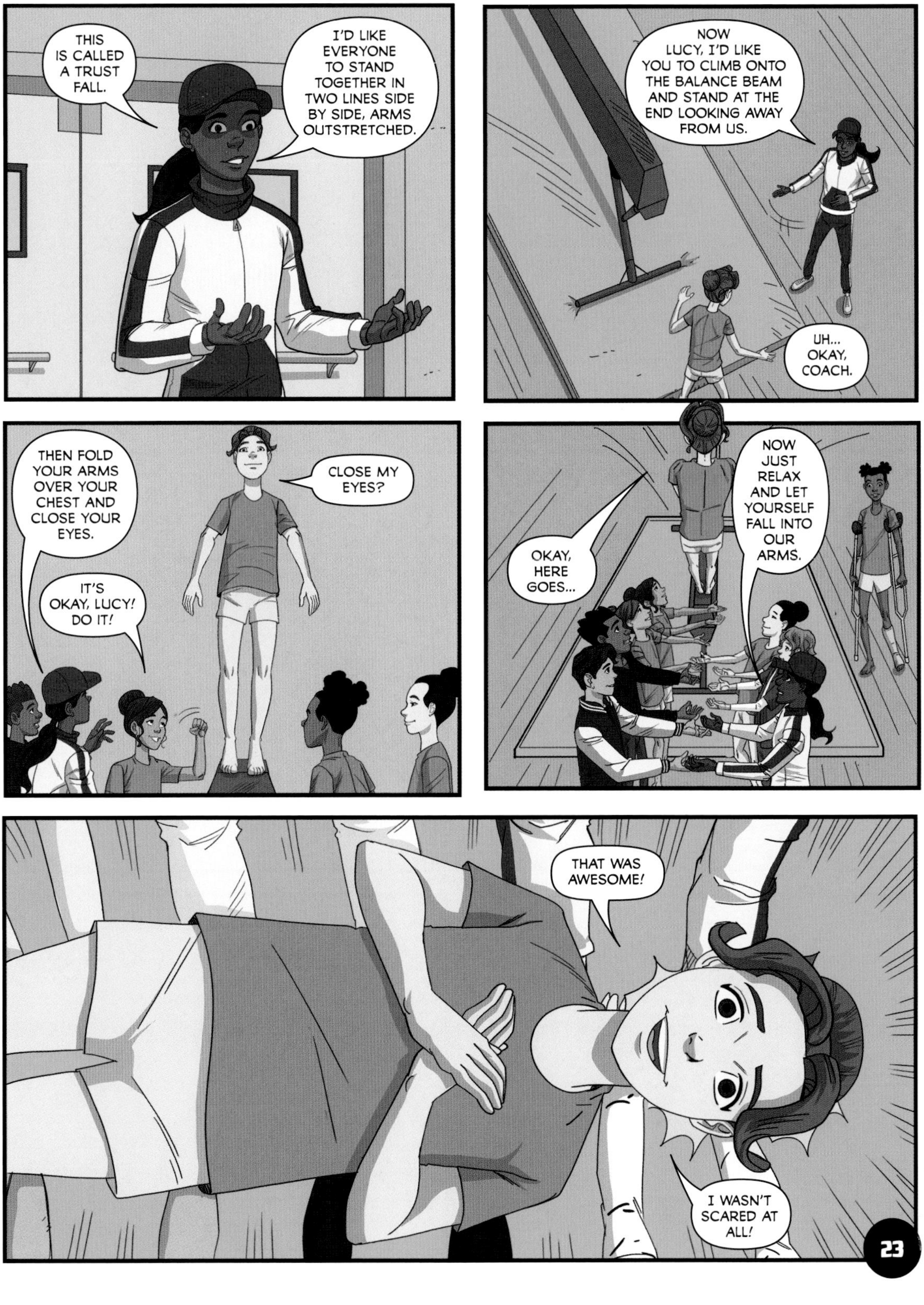
THIS IS CALLED A TRUST FALL.
I'D LIKE EVERYONE TO STAND TOGETHER IN TWO LINES SIDE BY SIDE, ARMS OUTSTRETCHED.
NOW LUCY, I'D LIKE YOU TO CLIMB ONTO THE BALANCE BEAM AND STAND AT THE END LOOKING AWAY FROM US.
UH... OKAY, COACH.
THEN FOLD YOUR ARMS OVER YOUR CHEST AND CLOSE YOUR EYES.
CLOSE MY EYES?
IT'S OKAY, LUCY! DO IT!
OKAY, HERE GOES...
NOW JUST RELAX AND LET YOURSELF FALL INTO OUR ARMS.
THAT WAS AWESOME!
I WASN'T SCARED AT ALL!

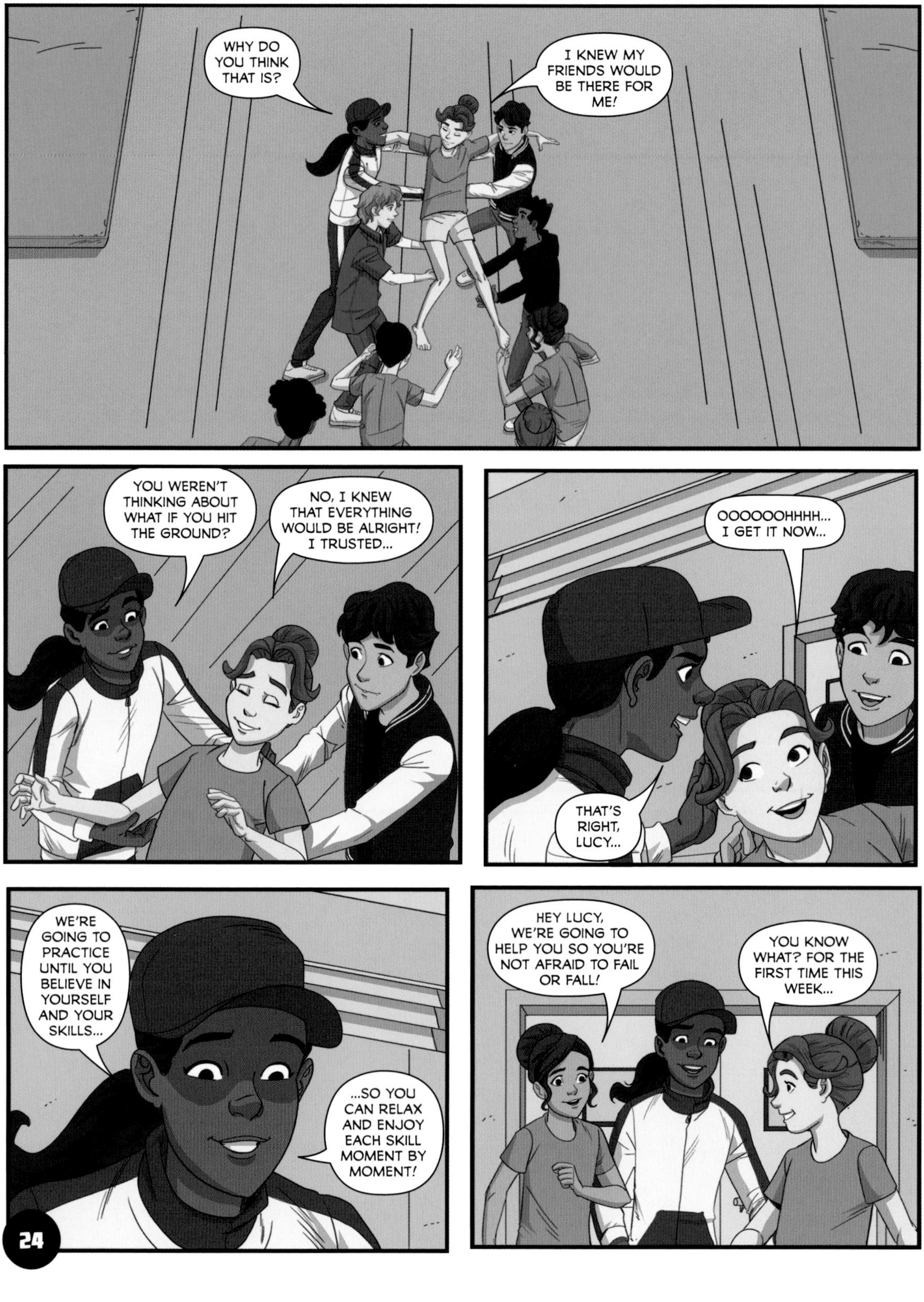
WHY DO YOU THINK THAT IS?
I KNEW MY FRIENDS WOULD BE THERE FOR ME!
YOU WEREN'T THINKING ABOUT WHAT IF YOU HIT THE GROUND?
NO, I KNEW THAT EVERYTHING WOULD BE ALRIGHT! I TRUSTED...
OOOOOOHHHH... I GET IT NOW...
THAT'S RIGHT, LUCY...
WE'RE GOING TO PRACTICE UNTIL YOU BELIEVE IN YOURSELF AND YOUR SKILLS...
...SO YOU CAN RELAX AND ENJOY EACH SKILL MOMENT BY MOMENT!
HEY LUCY, WE'RE GOING TO HELP YOU SO YOU'RE NOT AFRAID TO FAIL OR FALL!
YOU KNOW WHAT? FOR THE FIRST TIME THIS WEEK...

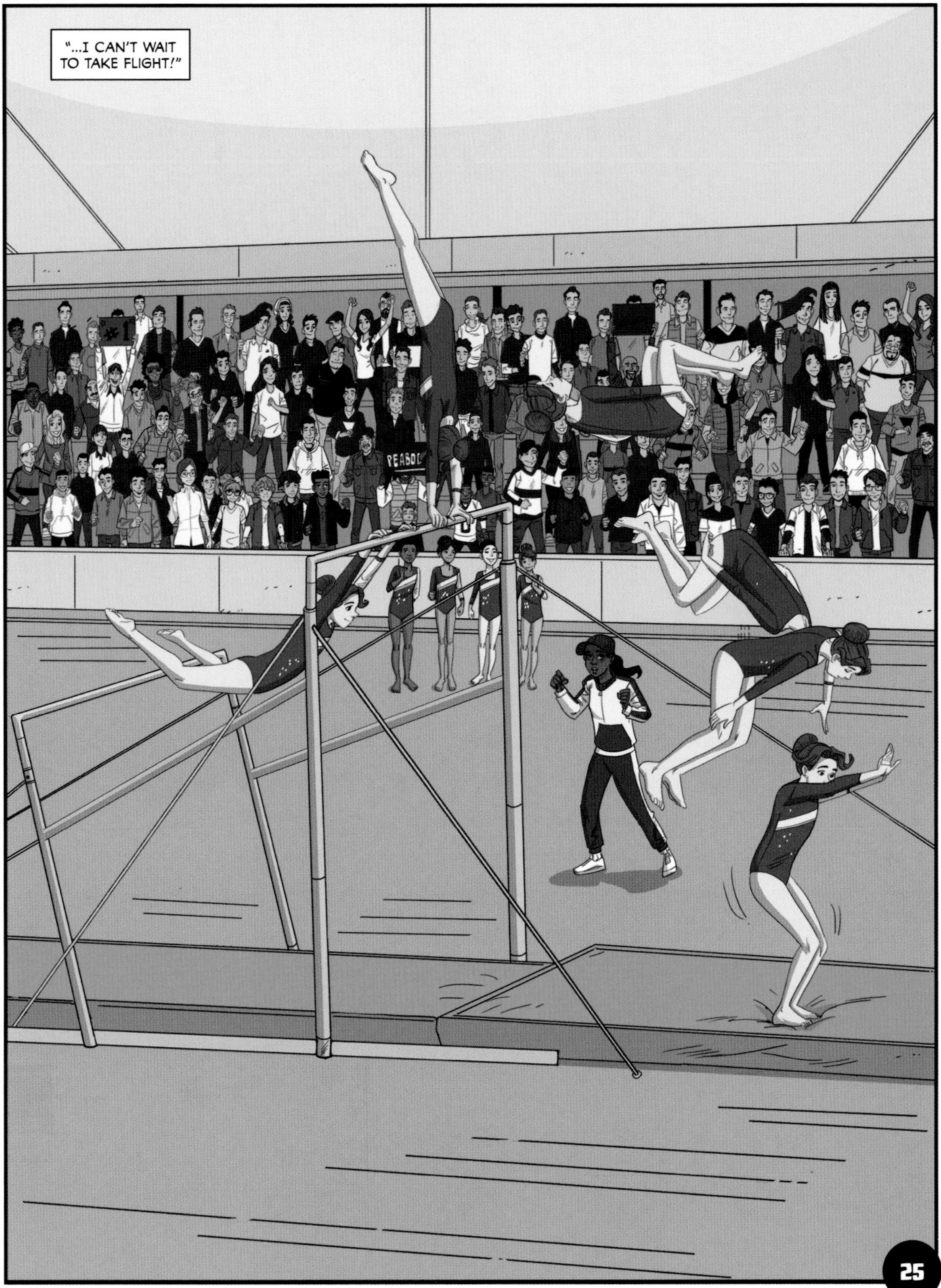
"...I CAN'T WAIT TO TAKE FLIGHT!"
#1

LUCY &

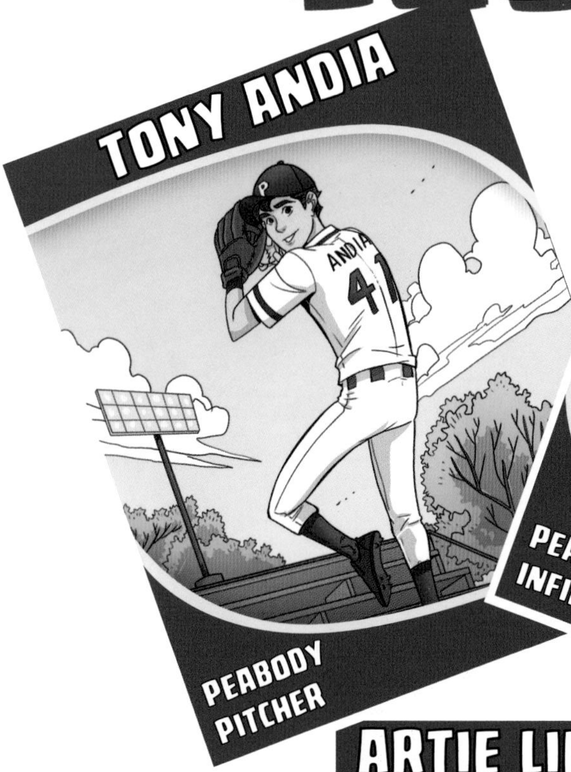
TONY ANDIA
PEABODY
PITCHER

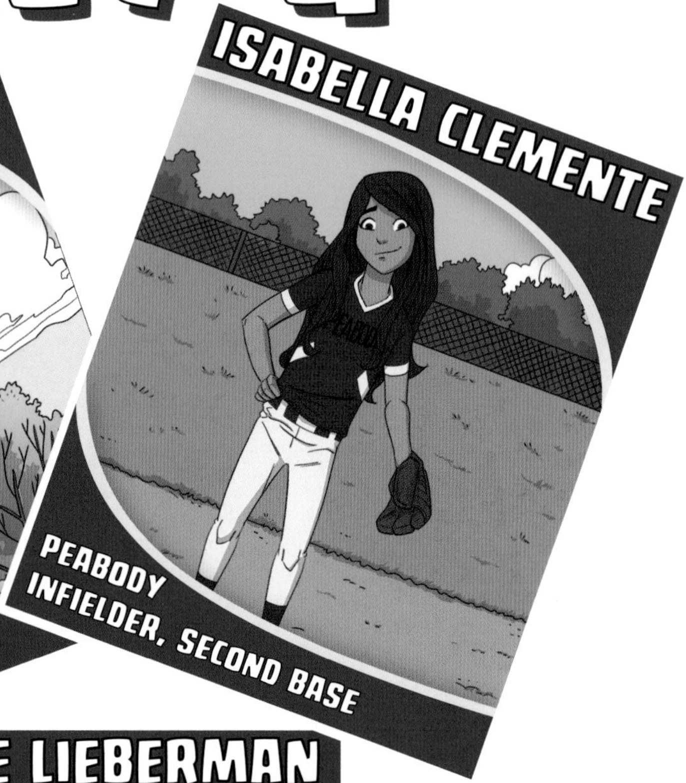
ISABELLA CLEMENTE
PEABODY
INFIELDER, SECOND BASE

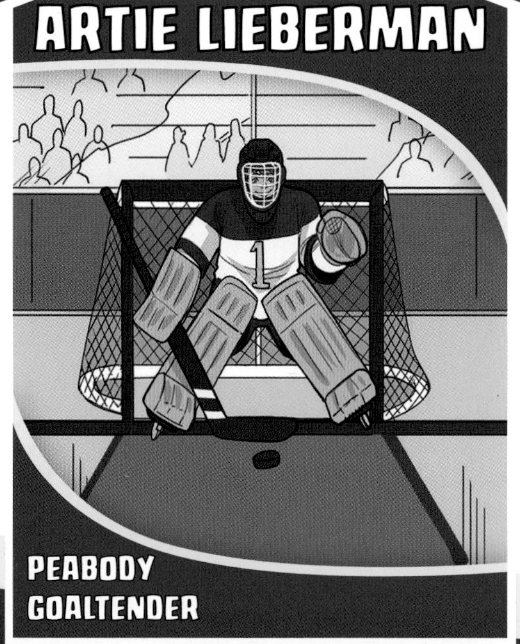
ARTIE LIEBERMAN
PEABODY
GOALTENDER

FRIENDS

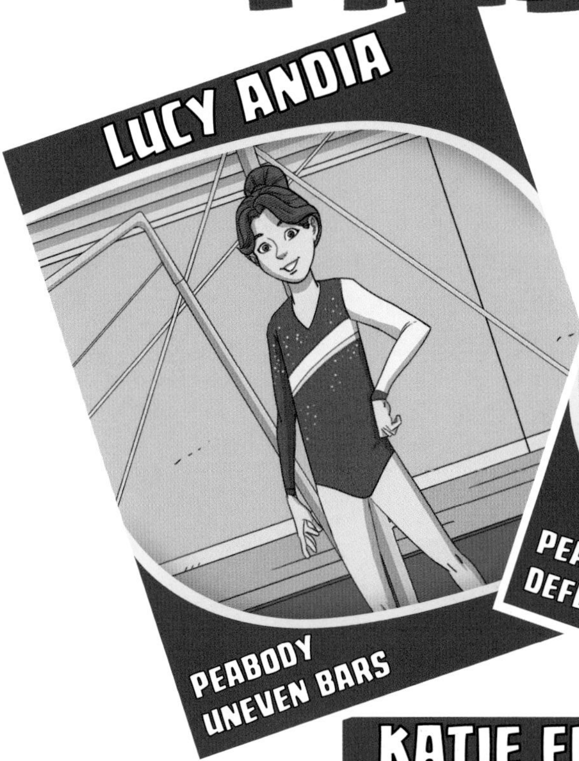
LUCY ANDIA
PEABODY
UNEVEN BARS

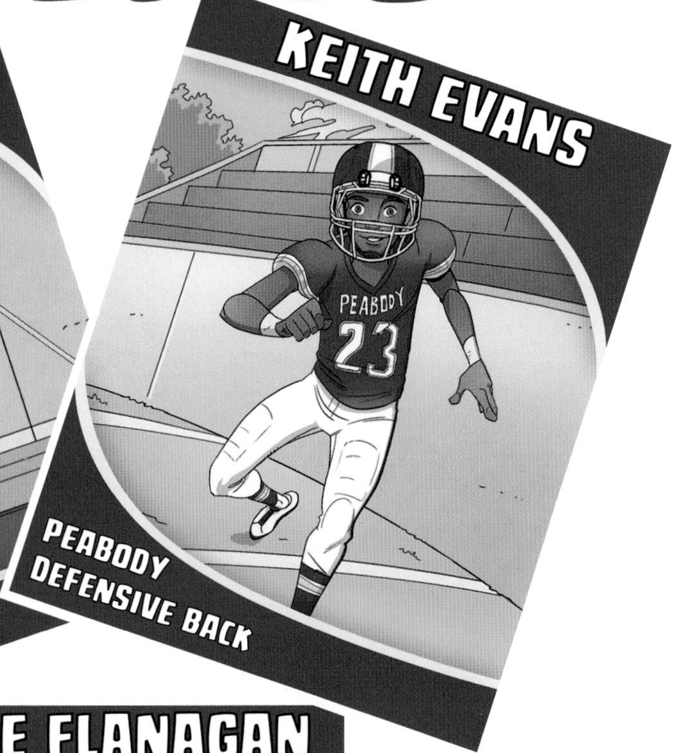
KEITH EVANS
PEABODY
23
PEABODY
DEFENSIVE BACK

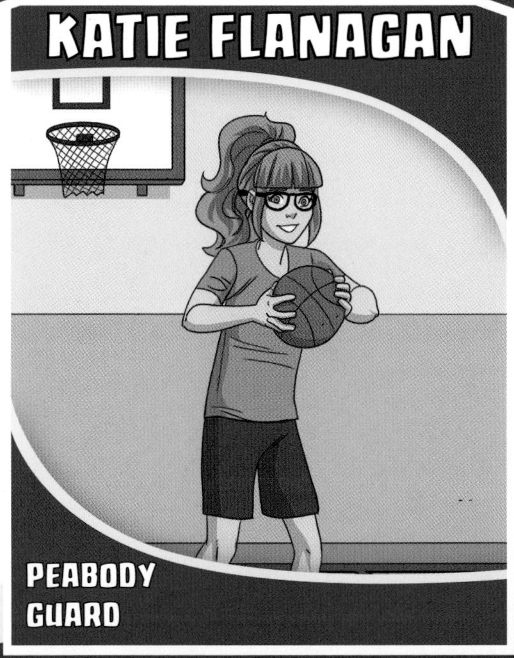
KATIE FLANAGAN
PEABODY
GUARD

GYMNASTICS

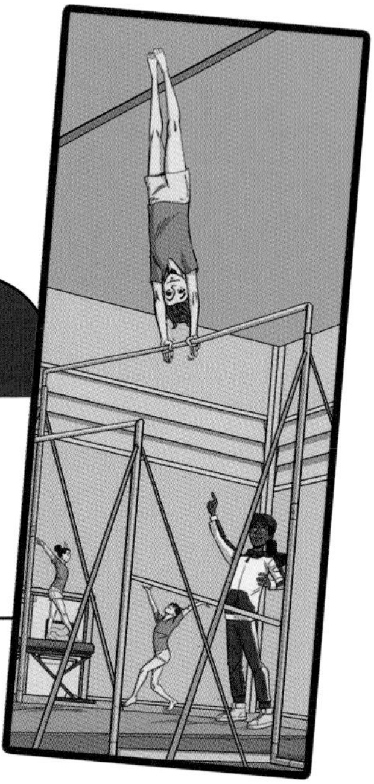

1. The uneven bars first appeared at the Summer Olympic games in which year?

a. 1902
b. 1952
c. 1992
d. 2012

2. Simone Biles is the most decorated gymnast in history. How many of her 35 medals are gold?

a. 7
b. 15
c. 27
d. 23

3. In uneven bars, the high bar is set at which height?

a. 250 cm (8.2 feet)
b. 200 cm (6.6 feet)
c. 150 cm (4.9 feet)
d. 100 cm (3.3 feet)

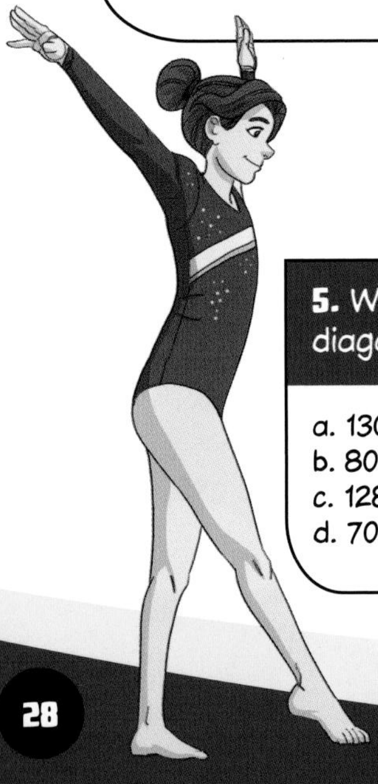

4. In uneven bars, the low bar is set at which height?

a. 270 cm (8.9 feet)
b. 170 cm (5.6 feet)
c. 70 cm (2.3 feet)
d. 17 cm (0.6 feet)

5. What is the range that is allowed for the diagonal distance between the two bars?

a. 130 cm (4.3 feet) - 190 cm (6.2 feet)
b. 80 cm (2.6 feet) - 103 cm (3.4 feet)
c. 128 cm (4.2 feet) - 192 cm (6.3 feet)
d. 70 cm (2.3 feet) - 140 cm (4.6 feet)

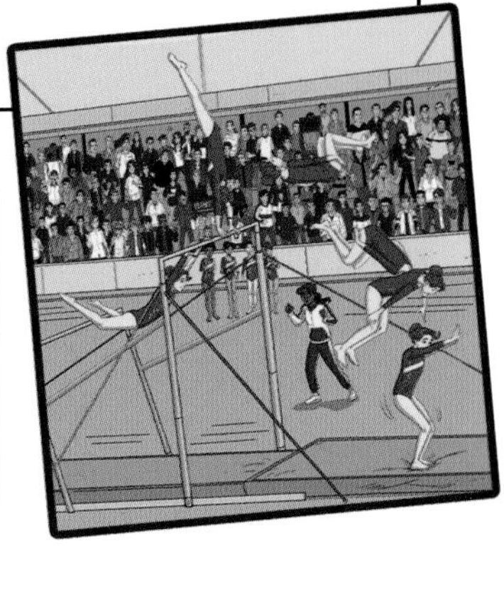

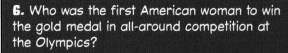

QUIZ

6. Who was the first American woman to win the gold medal in all-around competition at the Olympics?

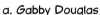

a. Gabby Douglas
b. Mary Lou Retton
c. Aly Raisman
d. Cathy Rigby

7. The apparatus called the uneven bars in the United States goes by a different name in the United Kingdom. There it's also known as the:

a. crooked bars
b. lopsided bars
c. asymmetric bars
d. misaligned bars

8. Which gymnast competing in uneven bars was the first to be awarded a perfect 10 in Olympic gymnastics competition?

a. Olga Korbut
b. McKayla Maroney
c. Nadia Comăneci
d. Laurie Hernandez

9. What does "New Life" mean in gymnastics scoring?

a. A gymnast gets to restart an event if he or she falls
b. A gymnast gets bonus lives if he or she gets a certain score
c. A gymnast has changed the country he or she represents
d. A gymnast's score does not carry over from one session to the next

10. Only one male gymnast has won the gold medal in all-around competition in both the Olympics and the World Championships. Who is he?

a. Paul Hamm
b. Bart Conner
c. Morgan Hamm
d. Kurt Thomas

WHAT DO YOU THINK?

There will be fear in life, but what's important is how you learn from it, prepare for it, and overcome it. That doesn't mean you get rid of it. You do your best in spite of it!

- What were two things Lucy was afraid of? Describe them using information from the story.

- What is something you're afraid of? Why do you think that is? What can you do to try to overcome your fear?

- Describe a time when your failure at something made you want to give up. Did you continue? If so, what helped you persevere? If not, what do you think kept you from continuing?

- Everyone needs support from others, both physical and emotional. Describe a time when you have received or given support to someone else. How did it feel?

- How is the trust fall an example of support? Explain how it is related to a team picking another player up. Explain what needs to happen inside a person's mind before attempting it.

GYMNASTICS FUN FACTS

1. The uneven bars began as men's parallel bars that were set at different heights. But this made moving from one to the other too easy. So the bars were moved farther apart to increase difficulty.

2. In order to get a better grip on the uneven bars, gymnasts apply chalk to their hands. People often sweat when moving or nervous, so it's good to have the best grip possible!

3. In artistic gymnastics, men and women compete in different events. Women compete in vault, uneven bars, balance beam, and floor exericse. Men's events are vault, pommel horse, parallel bars, still rings, horizontal bar, and floor exercise.

4. Simone Biles is considered by many to be the greatest gymnast of all time. But even she has had to work to improve her skills on the uneven bars! It's the only event in which she hasn't earned a gold medal!

5. In 1972, Olga Korbut invented the Korbut Flip. This move involved standing on the high bar, doing a back somersault, then grabbing the high bar again. This move thrilled crowds! But it was banned when judges declared it was too dangerous.

GLOSSARY

comps – A competition.

flyaway – A skill that appears to have a gymnast flying away from the bar.

kip – A way of getting on the bar in a front support position, or a handstand from a hanging or standing position.

momentum – Strength or force built up by motion or a series of events.

pike – A position where the body is bent only in the hips.

revolution – A progressive motion of a body around an axis.

routine – A combination of moves from start to finish.

tuck – A jump with the knees to the chest.

ANSWERS

1. b   2. c   3. a   4. b   5. a   6. b   7. c   8. c   9. d   10. a

ONLINE RESOURCES

Booklinks
NONFICTION NETWORK
FREE ONLINE NONFICTION RESOURCES

To learn more about gymnastics, perseverance, courage, and teamwork, please visit abdobooklinks.com or scan this QR code. These links are routinely monitored and updated to provide the most current information available.